Clutch

SIGNIFICANT BROTHERS #5

E. DAVIES

Publisher's Note: This is a work of fiction. Names, characters, places, and incidents are a product of the author's imagination. Locales and public names are sometimes used for atmospheric purposes. Any resemblance to actual people, living or dead, or to businesses, companies, events, institutions, or locales is completely coincidental.

Clutch / E. Davies. – 1st ed.
ISBN: 978-1-912245-16-1

Clutch

Prologue

ALEC

"You won't tell anyone, though, man?"

"We're cool, bro. You don't tell, I won't." Alec's response was automatic, after years of working around this kind of guy. The guys who were too manly for their own good, and terrified of the media finding out their big, bad secret.

Why couldn't he have been a physical therapist for actors? But no, he had to do sports physical therapy. So he kept his own… homosexual tendencies, as his parents used to put it… on the down-low.

Not like Gordon couldn't have asked for discretion *before* Alec was kneeling in front of him on the bedroom floor, but better late than never.

Satisfied again, Gordon pressed a hand to the back of Alec's head. His cock stood hard and straight, and looked impossibly tempting, even under its latex sheath. Alec's eyes were drawn to it, and then his tongue.

As he licked his way up the shaft, Gordon moaned in the back of his throat, then grunted, "Yeah."

Gordon wouldn't stand within two feet of him if anyone

else was around, but now? Alec just hoped Gordon didn't share this mansion with anyone else. If someone else walked in…

Gordon's leg was nearly back to perfect health. Alec was a football in front of the punter. He pushed away the thought of Gordon panicking and drop-kicking him across the room, before he laughed and ruined the mood. He had some serious sucking to do.

However much Alec told himself that he wouldn't look twice at athletes again—especially his own former clients—he seemed to find himself here too often.

A man had needs. Unfortunately, the particular need these guys met only ever lasted about fifteen minutes before they bundled him out the door. He had a policy against regretting hookups, but sometimes, a guy wanted a little wining and dining.

Far be it from him to look down on them for their choices, though. He was pretty damn closeted himself.

Who the hell would hire a gay physical therapist?

Definitely not his bread-and-butter clients—down in Tennessee, that was football and motorsports. Both big teams of big guys with big egos… who paid big money for a guy with Alec's reputation.

The last thing Alec needed was to ruin his career now. If rumors started flying, guys would wonder if he was touching them more than he needed to.

That meant, at the very least, way more muscle tension to contend with, meaning he couldn't do his job, and then he wouldn't get more business.

So Alec poured his time into his work and, off-hours, made do with guys who snuck in his back door.

"Yeah, baby. Suck it." It was the second time Gordon had

grunted the phrase, and it was no more appealing this time around. He didn't even sound very interested in the actual sucking going on—just in sounding like a porn star.

He loved giving head, but he suspected he wouldn't be getting any in return. And with Gordon's attitude, he sure as hell wouldn't be letting him try anything else. That *wannabe porn star* attitude never made for a satisfying fuck, so he wasn't gonna stick around and be disappointed.

He'd probably get more satisfaction from a good run around the block later, anyway.

Now that Alec had decided to finish the job orally, he doubled down on it. His hand squeezed the base of Gordon's shaft, his fingers wrapped around the rim of the condom to keep it in place.

"Oh, God, yeah. I'm gonna fuck your mouth. Gonna come so hard, baby."

Alec found himself relieved that his jaw would get a break soon. As much as he loved giving head, Gordon wasn't the most interesting guy in the world—and he wasn't giving Alec enough feedback to make him forget the latex taste.

Why the hell had he agreed to this? A hunk looked him in the eyes and he fell over himself to say yes. Every damn time.

Next time, I'll do better, he tried to promise himself. *For today, this is enough.*

CHAPTER

One

TYLER

"DEBRIS, BLOWN TIRE ON THE BACK STRAIGHT. YOU CAN PASS 45 on the inside around the next turn, but watch for 67."

Tyler almost tuned out the chatter over the radio from his spotter as he threw every ounce of attention into the turn. If he got the angle wrong, every damn turn was a chance for someone else to sneak up the inside and jockey for position.

If he got it badly wrong, every turn was a chance for a 150mph crash, taking out not just himself, but the drivers around him.

This was the zone. This was his high. He was fucking flying, the car jolting around the turn.

The temperature steadily climbed. Still cool compared to later this summer, though. Most tracks were in the south, and conditions in the cars were grueling by the middle of the summer. Three hours or more in a 140° car, and he was one of the only people crazy enough to do it without a second thought.

He heard his spotter warn him about Richie, the driver of car 67, again. Richie was right behind, but fighting to cut into the other line.

Alarm bells went off in his head.

Richie had approached Tyler before the crash—muttered under his breath that he was gonna lose another sponsorship if he kept racing like shit.

Tyler hadn't taken the bait. Some guys got all amped up before a race, trash-talked the others to get into the zone. He'd always thought it was stupid, and there was no point in wasting energy on others.

Racing was the driver and his car at its simplest. Sure, there were pit crew mechanics, the team owner, spotters, a hundred people with some kind of investment in the race, but they didn't matter.

The only thing that mattered was closing a few critical inches in this deadly, high-speed ballet.

He had a shot at the championship this year. His points were looking good after several great finishes this season—and so were Richie's.

If he could take top-five in this race, that was good enough for him. The closer to the front of the pack, the more points. The more sponsorships. Despite what Richie said.

He didn't see it coming. Neither did his spotter. By the time his spotter started to yell in his ear, there was nothing Tyler could do. The car jolted with an impact, and then spun.

He flipped gracefully into the air, sky and walls and crowd blurring.

Wedged in place, only his head somewhat free, all he could do was try to control the adrenaline surge.

Everyone crashed. It was inevitable. He'd done it before.

Usually you walked away, got checked out by the infield team, and the car was back in the running—

The ground closed in before he could finish the thought.

Blackness.

Was this the infield care center? The sterile walls and curtains were distinctive. Was he at a race, then?

Tyler stirred, trying to lift his arm to rub a hand down his face. His arms wouldn't move. They were as heavy and leaden like his thoughts.

He was on painkillers, then. Goddammit. He must be badly hurt. No finishing out the race.

What race was it, anyway? He fought to think through the haze.

"Ty? Man, you're up." That was Josh—it had to be. His best friend came to every race in the Knoxville area. Luckily for them, Knoxville was pretty close to half a dozen tracks.

During racing season—ten months of the year—it was easy to make it to many of the speedways. And the support was nice. Especially when he crashed out.

"What...?" Ty started, trying to rub his face again. He looked down this time and grimaced. His arms were bandaged. He couldn't feel it properly, but he was pretty sure there was a dull ache in his leg, too... and sharp pain in his ribcage, despite the painkillers.

"You've got a concussion. Lie back and rest."

"Fuck," Tyler muttered, closing his eyes obediently. "How bad is it?" Josh didn't say anything. He opened his eyes, easily reading his best friend's face. If Josh wasn't telling him, the news was bad. "Fuuuuck."

"They think there's a couple broken bones. Maybe torn muscles. You've been in and out of it. You don't remember the crash?"

Tyler shook his head. Between practice, qualifiers, and actual races, day in and out, he was at the tracks. "Was it a race?"

"Oh, Jesus. You really don't remember," Josh muttered.

Ty glared. "Tell me."

"Yeah, it was. Three laps to go, some guy… well, we don't really know what happened. I think some guy nudged you, and your car just went…" Josh made a vague twisting hand motion in the air, more like a bird flying to freedom than a car.

Tyler winced. "How bad's the wreck?" When Josh grimaced, Tyler swore under his breath. Roger Marcson, the owner, was gonna be pissed.

He closed his eyes again, resting now that his head had decided to throb. "This ain't the end." If he could move his fingers and toes, that meant he still had them. Hell, drivers who lost them still found a way back into the game. "How long am I gonna be off?"

Josh grimly told him, "Gotta wait for them to figure out what's wrong before you know, man."

"Just banged up a bit, that's not the end of the—oh, fuck." Now that he'd lifted one leaden arm, the piercing pain told him it wasn't just a bang-up job he'd done on himself. Bruises were nothing, but these were torn muscles at best.

That's not gonna get me any action at the afterparty.

Tyler blew out a long sigh and closed his eyes.

When he opened them again, more doctors were there, and he was groggy. Where was Josh? Oh, there in the corner.

Actually, there were a lot of people. Roger was here now, along with one of the other drivers—Chess. Nice of them to check on him.

He closed his eyes again, letting the exhaustion and painkillers sweep him away.

CHAPTER
Two

ALEC

"Got another new guy for you next. Driver."

Alec stopped by the desk at his Knoxville physical therapy practice as his secretary, Rosie, flagged him down. "Oh yeah?"

He didn't turn down a lot of work. He'd never liked the idea of contracting with one team, or even one league. Variety was interesting, and not putting all his eggs in one basket was smart.

A surprising number of athletes lived, worked, or played near Knoxville. He'd expected to have to move to Nashville, but business was brisk here. He'd been told a good PT was worth his weight in gold—a compliment he was willing to accept.

Of all the nut jobs he worked with, race car drivers were some of the worst. They were stubborn shits, used to the freedom to do things their own way.

On the other hand, they could be surprisingly compliant. They'd do the work he told him to, if he could gain their trust that it would lead to them getting behind the wheel a little faster. Not all sportspeople were like that.

Drivers wouldn't hear a word of quitting. No matter how often they put their necks on the line, they were always eager to get back out and do it again. It made him shake his head sometimes, what they were willing to do for their sport. As far as Alec was concerned, life was too short even without hurling yourself around tracks at a couple hundred miles an hour.

Rosie hummed significantly. "Tyler Joseph." When he shook his head, she sighed and added, "Crashed out in a spectacular ball of fire and glory last week?"

"Sounds painful."

"Sounds like four sessions, *minimum.* The guy's barely recovered from a borderline concussion. He's been lying down for a week, and it sounds like he wants to jack the nearest car dealership just to get behind a wheel. His next race is next week. My unprofessional opinion says that's not going to happen, from his description of his injuries."

Alec raised his brow.

Rosie chuckled and clarified, "From what I interpreted of his description."

They always underestimated their injuries and down-played them. Throwing them behind the wheel too early was dangerous for everyone involved, but they were desperate to do it anyway.

Alec knew what this meant: convincing the guy to stay sidelined. An impossible task. "Ouch. Wish me luck."

"Luck. He's waiting in room three." Rosie winked, inexplicably.

That usually meant the client was hot and maybe gay.

Oh, good. Another one.

Alec shook his head and walked to room three at a brisk stride.

Rosie clearly knew more than she was letting on, but he tried to stay professional. He didn't proposition clients—and if they propositioned him, he never let anything happen at work. Still… he wasn't *really* out.

And then he saw the man who was waiting for him in room three.

Oh, God. Not again.

He was the boy next door, but gorgeous. Knee-bucklingly gorgeous. With the slow, sincere smile that meant he knew he was gorgeous, but he wasn't wrapped up in himself.

"Tyler?"

He was met with a blinding smile. Tyler had turned his charm on. "Alec Lands, right?"

"That's me." Alec shook his hand, unsurprised at the strength of his grip. He shut the door behind himself and moved for the tall-backed chair. "You've got yourself into a hell of a predicament. Tell me about it."

"Oh, pretty bad crash, they say." Tyler's smile faded into a glower. "Been off the track for a week now. Only yesterday did they let me get off bed rest and walk around."

"That's rough," Alec sympathized. "Let's grab your medical file."

"Oh, it's not as bad as they make it out to be." Tyler had that cocky attitude, too, like he was superhuman. But Alec spotted the way he sat, and the awkwardness of his leg and arm. Anyone surviving that kind of crash had to have known how damn lucky they were, even with today's allegedly improved safety standards. No wonder he had the attitude.

"Mmhmm. Torn muscles, fractured ribs, swollen ankle, and an arm that—oh, that's a hairline fracture." Alec glanced from the computer to Tyler. "But let me guess: you wanna get behind the wheel next week."

Tyler's expression lit up. "Can I?"

"No." Alec wasn't beating around the bush. For all their faults, drivers were also used to hearing the honest truth instead of what they wanted to hear, and he had the sense Tyler was a straight-up guy.

Tyler took it well. He blew out a sigh, then shook his head. "Figures. Week after? I can't miss more than a couple races in a row. Looks bad."

"I know. We're gonna test your strength today, and then I can give you an estimate. You might not like it," Alec warned him.

"I might not listen," Tyler corrected him and grinned. The way he was smiling was more than friendly. Was he hitting on him?

"You don't listen, you stay out of the races for longer," Alec told him flatly. "And your points suffer."

That hit home. Tyler sucked in a breath, then nodded. "What do I have to do?"

Alec nodded at his table. "Hope those shorts are loose."

"Looser than me after a couple beers," Tyler promised, winking at him as he shifted from the chair to hop up on the table.

Alec's cheeks flushed, and it was all he could do to stay professional. "Good. I wanna see your range of motion in both arms and legs. The ribs—I'm sure you know that's a hell of an injury."

"Yeah. Not a lot you can do for ribs," Tyler agreed.

Somehow, one guy seemed to take up all the space in the room. It was hard to avoid being drawn to him. There was a magnetic charm about him—a certain way he held himself, like he knew exactly who he was and what he wanted.

Alec told himself again to calm the fuck down. It was going to be a long hour if he didn't.

"Five more weeks? Not a fucking chance."

Tyler had behaved himself pretty damn well during the examination. Alec had started to get his hopes up that he could ignore the sparks that flew between them any time he touched Tyler's skin to move his arm this way or that.

"The work can't begin for real until the swelling finishes going down," Alec told Tyler, using the tone that meant he was not leaving room for debate. "It's almost there, so I'll see you again in two days. Then we start easy, make sure we don't aggravate any of those injuries."

"Easy is bullshit," Tyler muttered.

"You wanna get better, you're gonna have to follow orders."

Tyler's jaw firmed as he sat up slightly, then winced and let himself lie flat on his back again. Sitting up couldn't have been easy in his state, so Alec put a hand on his shoulder to encourage him to stay flat.

"I'm not good at following orders," Tyler told him. And then, it was back.

Alec had *almost* managed to forget the chemistry between them. The thin line between playful but professional and flirtatious was hard to judge.

It felt like every breath he took without kissing Tyler was a wasted opportunity. And Tyler's lips were wet and plump.

He kept licking them, especially when Alec touched him. It was distracting as fuck.

Alec didn't need to touch Tyler again, though, so he resisted all instinct and didn't. He tucked his hands in his pockets instead and shook his head. "We can do this the easy way or the hard way."

Tyler propped himself up on his elbows, his gaze half-lidded. "How about the hard way? How hard is it?"

Alec drew a breath to give Tyler the usual speech about professional boundaries, but Tyler beat him there.

"I know, I know. You're not gay." Tyler rolled his eyes.

Alec blinked at him. "It's… not that. I don't sleep with former patients." He mentally added, *Anymore.* Tyler didn't need to know that. "It's technically not ethical, but more importantly, it never ends well."

"What about current patients?" Tyler gave him his best charming grin, and Alec laughed as he shook his head.

"Even worse."

"Damn." Tyler pouted. "I blew my chance the moment I met you?"

Alec eyed Tyler as he took a step back, and the air seemed to rush into the room again. He sat in the computer chair, the space giving his brain enough power to function again. "What painkillers did you say you're on?"

Tyler groaned and swung his legs over the side of the table, kicking his feet like he'd been caught with a hand in the cookie jar. "It's not the drugs talking."

"Mmhmm." Alec winked. "I don't know that."

Tyler relented and shook his head. "Fine," he said, sliding his feet back into his sandals. "But it's a wasted opportunity, let me tell you. How many gay guys do you treat?"

Alec's lips twitched into a smile. "A lot. Way more than you'd expect. They just don't want the media to know."

Tyler's face clouded over, and he was suddenly very busy sorting out simple Velcro straps on his sandals. "Mmm."

"So, two days' time. Rosie will arrange the time with you, so stop by the desk on your way out."

Tyler nodded, straightening up again. He offered his hand to shake and Alec took it, only to find his hand swept up. Tyler kissed the back of his hand playfully. "Charmed."

Alec laughed and pulled his hand away. This guy was gonna be way more than a handful. "Go on, scram."

"Yes, sir." Tyler winked and saluted with a finger, then sauntered out of the examination room.

Alec had to take a few deep breaths when the door closed behind him. He had the four o'clock patient to see, which meant storing away the memory of warm, soft lips against the back of his hand.

Putting it somewhere he could access it later, when he took a shower after work.

Yeah. That was going to be an awesome shower.

CHAPTER

Three

TYLER

"I MEAN, IT'S NOT EVEN FUCKING FAIR. RICHIE AIN'T SOME amateur. One tap shouldn't have sent me corkscrewing through the air like a—like a—"

Tyler stopped mid-gesture, his hands plucking at the sky for the right word.

"Like a corkscrew?" Josh's shit-eating grin was not the consolation Tyler might have hoped for.

"Yeah. Like a corkscrew. Fucking useful, bro. Thanks."

"You're welcome." Josh laughed loudly as he brought the axe down on a piece of wood. He was splitting firewood to stockpile in the lean-to attached to his cabin for next winter.

It wasn't the worst place to lie around, if he had to lie around anywhere and recover. The dude ranch Josh ran was low-stress, but it would have been a lot more fun if he could do anything.

He couldn't even chop the damn firewood. Hell, he couldn't stand and watch like usual—Josh had dragged out a chair for him.

Tyler groaned and rocked back on two legs of the chair.

"He said I won't be getting to the next race, that's for damn sure."

"Sucks." Josh winced sympathetically. "You being paid?"

"Not like I would be if I were racing," Tyler grumbled. "And I lost one sponsorship last year. I don't need to lose one again this year."

He didn't really need a reminder that last year hadn't been his best season. He'd been distracted with… well, his friends, for one thing. The endless sprawl of single life ahead of him, if he were lucky, for another.

It wasn't easy watching his best friends fall in love, knowing he was between a rock and a hard place if he ever wanted love himself.

Tyler shook his head. "I'm *not* losing another," he changed his sentence, dropping the chair to all four legs again. "Whatever the fuck Hanson thinks."

The drivers on the Hanson team—Richie, who had fucked up badly enough to nearly kill him, and the other three—had been insufferable this season, since getting the sponsorship he'd lost last year. It was almost enough to make him wonder if it was a deliberate attempt to hurt him.

And he *had* hit on Richie a year or so ago, at an afterparty, when it had seemed for all the world like Richie was making a pass at him. Then, Richie had backed off so fast he'd nearly fallen over himself to flee.

But that wasn't enough for a death grudge. And Tyler hadn't made enemies more than any other driver did. He didn't swear at his competitors or make rude gestures at them. He didn't bump draft, and he'd never even tried to cheat.

There was no reason anyone should dislike him, except

for being pretty, young, and in a fast car, and that described most of them.

"You ever thought about not getting back into the seat?" Josh tossed the freshly-split wood on the pile. "Maybe not killing yourself?" He cast Tyler a concerned look. "You looked like hell in the… whatever they call it. Field center."

"And that's why I'm not dating," Tyler muttered under his breath.

"What?"

"Nah." Tyler tried to wave it off.

"No," Josh insisted, propping his axe on his shoulder. "Why aren't you dating? Because you're a driver?"

"No. Because nobody would put up with me going to work, not sure if I'll come home." Josh was giving him a look like he was an idiot—Tyler was very familiar with these looks by now. "What?"

"You just described like a dozen different careers, dude. People date cops, firefighters, truck drivers, garbage men. God, fishermen. Loggers. You name it. Get over yourself and try it out." Josh smirked. "You know there's like, a hundred ladies who would do you in a second. Statistics say there should be, what, two to five guys? If you haven't fucked them all already."

Tyler scowled at him and flipped him off.

"You're not that ugly, and us guys are pretty easy. Maybe ten."

Tyler tried to ignore Josh. "Yeah, and dating and fucking isn't the same."

"True. So go date some of them after you fuck them. Or before. I don't care," Josh laughed.

"Most of those careers—people who can deal with a husband going off to work and maybe not coming home—

they're heroes, or whatever. Mine isn't that. I'm not doing it for glory and saving other people. I'm just an idiot in a car."

Josh hummed. "But you look sexy in the fire suit."

"Fuck you." Tyler laughed. "Anyway, it's all kind of pointless to think about. You know what the media would say. Even today, we don't have anyone big who's out. We have pretty well-known down-low gay guys, sure. I've slept with them already. But they're never, ever coming out. Not as long as they want sponsorship."

Josh couldn't argue with that. He sighed, rubbing his neck as he gazed over the fields, clearly trying to come up with an argument. Then, he shook his head and grabbed another log to split.

"You *know* I'm right," Tyler smirked. "And besides, I'm not putting myself through that hell for nothing."

"It wouldn't be for nothing."

Tyler rolled his eyes. "For some boyfriend, yeah. True love and everything."

"You wait 'til it happens to you," Josh laughed. "It's always at the worst time possible."

"Says the chronically single guy," Tyler pointed out.

"That's what everyone else says. And they should know." Josh had him there. The rest of their friendship group—seriously, all four of the six guys—had found boyfriends in not even a year. Several of them were engaged now.

Which left him and Josh as the sad, lonely, single outsiders. If one looked at it that way. If, instead, one chose to think about the no-strings-attached sex and parties every week? It wasn't a bad outlook for him.

Tyler just felt bad for Josh, who worked from dawn 'til dusk at the farm and rarely had time to meet eligible guys.

He deserved better, but he'd never stop and take time for himself.

"Why can't you come out? The media cares less these days," Josh finally said, after a few minutes of peace and quiet punctuated only by the sharp chopping sounds of his axe.

"Because—Jesus. We're talking southern states, right?" Tyler shook his head. They were both Tennessee boys, born and raised, so they knew as well as anyone the likelihood of being shunned as a pariah for something out of their hands. "They'd have a field day. My image would be gone. No more sponsorships means less money, more chance they'll yank me from the car. If they don't already do that, after I fucking totaled it, I'll count myself *lucky*. I don't need to add any more stress to the situation."

Josh had paused again, setting his axe aside. "What happens when you meet someone who'd be bad for your image but good for the real you?"

Tyler couldn't answer that one. He didn't want to, because he had the horrible, sneaking suspicion the answer wouldn't make him look good. He looked away, over the fields and toward the guest cabins.

Josh read into his silence. "Yeah. Being the perfect southern gentleman for the cameras is one thing. Being a monk because you're not allowed to chase a hot ass and the cameras are watching? And what about love? You gonna ditch that because you can't afford to? When does it stop?"

"Yeah." Tyler shook his head. He'd tried not to think that far ahead. Despite the bad season last year, his last couple years had attracted a lot of attention, and he didn't want to give that up. On the other hand, it made him a lot more vulnerable.

He'd never been closeted before racing. He just hadn't

brought it up directly on the track, all the way from his go-karting days as a kid, because work was work and home was home. Not everyone thought that way, of course. Some drivers flaunted their trophy wives in order to get into the headlines more.

The right company *might* see him as an opportunity rather than a risk, but it was a hell of a big risk to overcome, too.

His team knew. He'd always seen that as enough. But was it?

Tyler blew out a sigh. "Why are we talking about some theoretical situation? I'm supposed to be getting pissed off that I broke myself, not that I don't have a good lay."

"Oh," Josh grinned. "We can talk about those if you'd rather."

He lived vicariously through Tyler's afterparties. He'd come as Tyler's best friend to a few of them, but out of consideration for Tyler, he'd never taken anyone home from them. Tongues would wag too easily, and suddenly Tyler would find himself in a tabloid article about wild gay threesomes.

"Anyone else decide they want a walk on the wild side with you?" Josh pressed.

Tyler's sexuality wasn't quite at open secret status yet, but word had to be getting around by now. He knew damn well that he was living on the knife's edge, but that was the point of life. The thrill of the race, the chase, or nearly getting caught. Adrenaline. The rush of victory or the bittersweet taste of loss.

If you didn't live a lot, why bother living at all? He tried not to apply his life philosophy to his dating life. That was different, he told himself. Josh couldn't be right about every single thing, all the time.

And that definitely wasn't a pang of loneliness that stabbed through him whenever he watched couples on their honeymoon, wandering around the ranch like they had eyes for nobody but each other.

Tyler bit his tongue, his sigh lost in the crack of splitting wood. "So, there was this guy a couple weeks ago who wanted to drink champagne off me."

If he wasn't good for anything else, he might as well tell a good story.

Four

ALEC

EVENING WAS ALEC'S LEAST FAVORITE TIME OF DAY. DURING the day, he had patients to distract him. But during the evening, his house was much too quiet. His mind often started to wander, and that was dangerous.

He'd told himself for years that he was too busy to take on any new hobbies or socialize much. When he tried, he never seemed to stick with it, and he didn't even know why.

Sometimes he headed out to bars, but even when he'd been just twenty-one and up to his neck in anatomy home-work, escapism had never appealed to him. The older he got, the less he wanted to waste his time getting drunk and making a fool of himself.

The problem was, there didn't seem to be much alternative if he wanted friends—or even a lover.

Alec fought back the tide of bitterness that threatened to swamp him once again. Every now and then, it felt like he'd outed himself—and lost half his life in the process—for nothing.

What did it matter if he was gay, if he now had no family *and* no boyfriend to commiserate with?

"Okay, I gotta get out of the house," he grumbled. When this mood took him, he was better off outside, anywhere at all, than home alone.

Alec tugged on his running shoes. It was a Tuesday evening, which meant the Knoxville gay men's running group was out for a gentle run in Lakeshore Park. But if he got seen running with a gay group…

It was a bittersweet irony. He was *just* out enough to lose the support around him, but not out enough to take pride in who he was. If he wanted to keep his business, he couldn't dance on any floats. Hell, he couldn't even casually mention his personal life like his clients and colleagues did.

He told himself he wasn't ashamed, but where was his pride?

Carried away by his thoughts, Alec strode out the door and jogged down to the sidewalk, then broke into a run.

The first mile was always the hardest. It took time to find a rhythm—time to figure out the smooth connection—even interplay—between his heartbeat and his legs.

He found himself steering for Lakeshore Park before he knew it, pushing aside all his fears. If he got a move on, he could make it in time. Worst came to worst, he could say he was there to do research for a client.

"Come on. You can do it," Alec panted between steps, ignoring the pedestrians who edged further away from him. "You can fucking make friends."

He arrived just in time—it looked like the guys in the group had just finished stretching.

"Ah, hello." A long, lean fellow with the classic runner build stretched out a hand to shake. "Welcome."

That's it? No questioning me? Alec was a little taken aback. He'd expected to be interrogated on… on what, he didn't know. His gay credentials? But the group was just waving slightly to him, some guys nodding and others waving. Everyone seemed busy contemplating the trail they were about to run.

This kind of worked for Alec. The less asked, the better. He jerked his chin in nods to everyone who nodded to him as he stretched.

They took off en masse, quickly splitting into groups of three or four. His thighs burned at first, but the group quickly settled into a gentle pace. He was tempted to push himself to join a group near the front, but he had to get back home after this.

Alec found himself with a couple who were more interested in chatting to each other than him, which worked just fine for him.

There was a strange, new-to-him sense of community from being among other gay guys without having to talk about himself or justify his choices.

Alec's spirits lifted. Only slightly, but even a slight lift beat his last few months. Something had shifted so subtly, almost imperceptibly, in his mind.

Instead of worrying about where he'd find his eventual boyfriend or even life partner, and how he was going to navigate that, why not see what came as it came? He couldn't stop the right man from walking into his life—or his office, perhaps—and he didn't want to.

When that happened… well, he wasn't going to avoid or hide the person who was worth it. That would be choosing the closet, far more so than he did even right now.

The rhythmic slapping of his feet on the ground drew

him through the worst of his thoughts, especially when he wondered if that would even ever be a problem. The guys he seemed to attract never seemed to want him long-term.

Maybe he'd meet someone like Tyler, only... *out* and *available*, and not one of his clients.

Alec had heard of the ideas of drawing his ideal man closer to him. Visualization and all that shit. He was way too busy to try that, but it wasn't a bad idea to figure out what exactly it was that drew him to a man, so he could keep an eye out for that kind of guy in the future.

Cheeky, definitely. Willing to push back and hold his ground. He definitely had to be as stubborn as Alec. Alec had to be stubborn on the job all too often, and he could run roughshod over a meek, quiet guy. Someone with a big heart but a joking sense of humor. Alec didn't see the point in being grim and solemn all the time, like life was all about who could be the most serious.

Someone who was driven and passionate, though, was important. Alec didn't mind what they were passionate about, so long as they had *a* passion. Like his own fascination with the human body, but perhaps in another field.

Shut up, he told his brain when it tried to hint at the obvious. There were, after all, plenty of guys who came into the office fitting that description. So why pick one guy—one random guy, of the many—to crush on?

No. That wouldn't do.

Alec sped his pace up, nodding at his companions as he left the couple to be coupley and joined the front runners.

One of them jerked his chin at Alec, but that was all the acknowledgment he got—or wanted. He was here to run and forget himself. The front runners all seemed to agree.

All that mattered was his sweat. Measured breaths. Footsteps on the path.

His heart rate.

It was hammering *almost* as fast as when Tyler Joseph had walked into his office.

Goddamn it. Rosie had been right—Tyler was exactly his type. She was getting scarily good at assessing who was. She never said a word. She didn't have to. She could just wink, and Alec would get all flustered and she would laugh in his wake as he hurried off to treat them like a professional.

After his experience with Gordon, Alec had been trying to take it easy. Trying not to fall all over the first guy who looked at him the right way. That wasn't the path to true happiness, he was pretty sure.

His body remembered it without warning: warmth, pressure on the back of his lips. The sneaky smile that Tyler had worn when he kissed his hand, like he'd known damn well what effect it would have on Alec, and was willing to push his luck.

The little asshole. He was probably going to try to leverage that into permission to do some dumbass stunt like take part in the next race.

Not a chance. Alec was going to have to push back against him, he could already tell.

If only that weren't so damn appealing.

Goddamn. He was running out of energy to run from the simple truth: he was attracted to Tyler, and so long as Tyler was on extra-strength painkillers and making eyes at him, he was going to have to ignore it for everyone's good.

He would have sighed, if he'd had breath to spare. Sometimes, being a professional fucking sucked.

Not that Tyler was his type, normally. He *looked* like the

boy next door, but he acted like the guy who'd taken several poles and first-place finishes and collected a lot of points for his age.

Tyler wasn't the biggest household name yet, but given enough time? If he kept it up? He would be smack dab in the center of the spotlight.

Exactly where Alec didn't want to be. He had too much to lose—and so did Tyler.

Keep your distance. That's the only way this will end well.

CHAPTER

Five

TYLER

"I'll pick you up in an hour, yeah?" Josh cast Tyler a worried glance. "Sure you don't want company?"

Tyler reminded himself to play it cool. If he got his way, he was gonna be Alec's last appointment of the day for good reason. "I'll text you. Might have a meeting after this."

God bless him, Josh never asked. He just smirked at Tyler. "Mmhmm. Meeting. Get your ass out of here."

Tyler waved and stumbled out of the car, making his slow way toward the front door of the physical therapy clinic. He was determined to look better than he felt.

By the time he made it to the waiting room, Rosie had already pushed the button to swing the door open for him.

"Thank you, ma'am," Tyler said. He winked to cover up the impulse to frown from the ache in his bones. "And good afternoon!"

"Hi again, Tyler. Water?"

Tyler shook his head. "I'm fine, thanks." Before he could ease himself into a chair, she showed him to an examination room.

"All right. Alec will be in to see you in a couple minutes." She wasn't fussing, which he appreciated. He might have been busted up, but the last thing he needed was a reminder.

"Thanks, Rosie." He flashed her his trademark smile, but she didn't blush or giggle—just grinned back at him and closed the door on her way out.

Huh. Was she immune to the charming Ty grin? That was a new one. Tyler was used to getting his way with it.

Before he could read much into it, the door opened again and he glanced up, expecting to see Rosie.

It was Alec, looking breathtaking in a crisp, pressed shirt and billowing white jacket. That roguish half-smile was back as he nodded in greeting, and Tyler's eyes couldn't seem to find anything but those plump lips.

The sight wiped Ty's brain of thoughts, clean as a fresh air filter. Still didn't stop him saying the first thing that came out of his mouth. "I'm back. Uh. Obviously." So much for filters. He flushed and clamped his mouth shut before he could say anything else dumb.

"Hi. Good to see you again," Alec answered, his eyes twinkling. He was clearly being considerate by not commenting on Tyler's sudden inability to form sentences.

"Hi," Tyler answered, since he'd forgotten to say it before. Oh, God. This was going to be a hell of an hour if this was the way it was starting. "Unfortunately, I'm still a current patient. I aim to change that, though."

"Let me guess. You want to recover and get back behind the wheel in three seconds," Alec said, his lips quirking into a smile. "Sure haven't heard that before."

Tyler snorted. "Nah. Just aiming to avoid your, what is it… ethics clause." The quizzical look Alec shot him made him add, "You might have lots of patients, but I don't have a lot of patience."

Alec finally cracked a grin, gesturing for him to sit on the table. "Oh, we're picking up where we left off?"

"You bet. It was just getting good." Tyler winced, then bit his lip to keep his face straight as he lay back on the table.

It was all he could do to keep *all* of him lying flat, especially when Alec started manipulating his joints. Only the sharp sparks and waves of pain that coursed through him, making his hair stand on end and breath catch in his chest, kept him from reacting more physically to the warm hands on his bare skin.

If Alec noticed the swell in Tyler's pants, he didn't comment. "You're healing, but you want to avoid muscle atrophy in the meantime. We'll start you with some gentle exercises. Those ribs are going to be the worst part. How are your abs?"

"Killing me," Tyler admitted, grinning. "I won't be on my hands and knees for a while."

Alec murmured, almost too quietly to hear, "That's a shame. Strictly sleeping on your back, hm?"

Tyler caught his breath. Was Alec finally flirting back? *Please, please be flirting.* It was too painful to watch a guy who was exactly his type keep his distance. Alec might just be one more trophy on Tyler's mantel, but boy, would he be worth the effort to catch.

"Oho," Tyler murmured, smirking. "I just need to find guys with rock-hard thighs and make them do all the work."

"Core strength isn't to be underestimated." Alec was biting back a laugh as he gently moved Tyler's arm up as far as he could go before Tyler started wincing.

Tyler hissed as white heat shot through his rib, making it hard to breathe in.

Alec quickly but steadily lowered his arm again. "Okay. That's not ideal. You can't reach up at all, hm?"

I can grab your ass instead of your head when we kiss. Tyler bit back the retort, but his gaze was fixed on Alec's lips again. The chemistry between them was dizzying, and it was only getting worse the longer Alec touched him non-sexually.

The strictly professional touches were starting to drive him fucking crazy. It was way too easy to imagine those long, delicate fingers wrapping around his shoulders while Alec's legs wrapped around his back, breathed whimpers becoming a soundtrack of pleasure.

Oh, God, what he wouldn't give to heal faster. In this shape, he was gonna be stuck watching Alec ride him.

Don't get ahead of yourself, he reminded himself quickly.

He wasn't going to count his twinks before they hatched. But this twink would look great riding him, jerking himself off, head thrown back in pleasure.

Oops. He was getting hard now, unable to pull his thoughts away from those sexy mental images.

"Ty," Alec tapped his shoulder, grinning at him. "I need you to focus, even if the painkillers are making everything fuzzy."

"I'm not on any."

Alec stared at him, clearly taken aback as those pretty lips opened and closed once. Then, he frowned. Even that disapproving expression was fucking hot. "Don't tell me you're going all macho on me."

"No. But you wouldn't let me hit on you when I was drugged up." Tyler gave him a grin that might have been a bit more woozy than he intended from the dull ache coursing through his body.

The way Alec laughed was suddenly warm and rich, not professional and polite. Alec's dimples appeared. God. Tyler desperately wanted to lean up, grab his lapels, haul him in for a kiss…

"I'm flattered," Alec murmured.

Tyler's stomach lurched, and he instinctively prepared himself for the speech: *I'm flattered, but I'm taken.* Or maybe *I'm flattered, but I'm straight.* Or *I'm just not into your type.*

But Alec didn't say any of those things. Instead, hesitation written on his face, Alec paused. He gently rested a hand on Ty's shoulder. "We shouldn't do anything while you're in a vulnerable position. While you're in treatment."

"It's not like you're my shrink, man." Ty squinted, trying to catch Alec's gaze. Suddenly, Alec seemed to look anywhere but him. "But yeah," he added, not wanting to reel him in too fast and lose the catch. "I see your position. How about I take you for a drink? I could use the company."

Alec looked surprised. "No strings attached?"

"Just a couple guys being buddies, swapping sports stories." Tyler smirked. "If we *happen* to hit it off and fuck all night, it's nothing to do with your workplace then."

Pink crept from Alec's neck up to his cheeks, and then he surprised Tyler by laughing and nodding. "Fine. As long as there's no expectations."

Tyler caught himself before he could say *really?* and give away his excitement. Instead, he grinned, his confidence carrying him through. "Great. Tonight work?" He carefully pushed himself upright, and Alec was there, helping him sit up again, his hands firm and warm and tempting.

I really gotta get laid. Preferably with him.

Tyler drew a quick breath, winced at the pain that instinctive reaction caused, then nodded his thanks.

"I'm free tonight," Alec said, his tone cautious.

Tyler didn't want to give him a chance to think harder about the decision. He gave Alec a trademark charming grin, and unlike Rosie, it seemed to work on him. Alec's dimples reappeared. "Perfect. Seven? Here's my card." He dug it out of his wallet and handed it over.

Alec skimmed the card, then pocketed it and nodded. "I'll text after work."

"Can't wait. I could really use a drink." Tyler grinned.

He was on his best behavior for the rest of the appointment, listening to the exercises he was given, but his mind was six hours in the future.

Does this count as a date? Is this the first date I've had in years?

No, he reminded himself. Not a date. Just hanging out and trying to charm his way into Alec's pants. He looked like he was worth the challenge.

And without a challenge, he was gonna go out of his mind.

"I can't believe you." Josh's hand covered his face, but his shoulders were shaking with laughter. "Only you could score a date while bashed and bandaged up, looking like crap."

Tyler pretended to be offended. "Looking like crap? Thanks, man." His movements to unbuckle were slow and calculated. The ibuprofen didn't do much for the ache throughout his whole torso. Overcompensating for his ribcage had taken its toll on his abs, as Alec had suspected. "That's not what he thought, if he said yes."

"You can't even brush your hair!"

Tyler winked. "Good thing I don't have much of it." He raised a hand slightly and waved. "I'll get a cab back, don't worry about me."

"I hope he's worth it." Josh grinned at him and pretended to slap his knee—his bad leg. Tyler instinctively flinched away before Josh snickered. "See? How are you even gonna— you know, I don't want to know, actually."

"Oh, I've thought it through. I have a plan. Wanna hear?"

"Keep it to yourself and get out of my car, you sex pest." Josh pretended to shove Tyler out of the car.

Tyler laughed as he eased himself onto his feet, leaning heavily on the good leg. He did his best to look stable and pain-free. Last thing he needed was Josh cock-blocking him. "Fuck off, Mr. Green Eyes of Jealousy."

Josh rolled his eyes and flipped him off. "Ain't jealousy, just facts. Have fun."

Tyler blew a kiss and limped away from the car, straight into the bar where he'd told Alec to meet him.

Despite his banter, there was a weird emotion running through him. The assortment of aches and pains that stabbed through him kept him from putting his finger on it until his hand slid on the cool metal of the door handle. His palms were damp.

I'm... nervous.

Okay, that was weird. Sure, he had the same adrenaline rush before a race as anyone else, but that quickly faded. He didn't have the concentration to spare to being nervous in the middle of a race—even a few hours or hundreds of laps in.

And picking guys up was never a big deal. There was always another discreet, sexy guy in the wings. He carefully kept himself from showing off guys in front of any media, but afterparties were another story.

It wasn't just fans—a surprising number of drivers were more flexible than they'd admit after a few drinks. Plus, every team had more than just the drivers. Between owners, pit crew, engineers, PR people, and everyone else involved in the industry, there was no shortage of guys out there, and a few of them were always willing to give him a second look.

Why get nervous about this one particular guy?

He strode in—or as close to striding as he could manage in his state, which was more of an undignified hobble.

"Over here." That was Alec's voice.

Tyler turned carefully and found Alec leaning out and waving at him from a corner booth of the bar. He was staying out of sight of the doorway. A private little spot. Perfect.

Alec nodded and headed over at a slow amble, pretending not to be in a rush even if he couldn't have possibly gone faster.

"Jesus. You're in a state." Alec's brows were pinched with concern. "I shouldn't have made you come out…"

Ty winked. "You ain't making me come out 'til the good night kiss. But I don't mind coming down here tonight, either."

Alec snorted with amusement and pushed a beer across the table to him. "Here." He covered the glass before Tyler could take it. "As long as you aren't on anything."

"Nothing much," Tyler grinned. "Thanks, man." He carefully picked up the beer with his good hand, and then toasted Alec. "To blossoming friendship."

Alec clinked, sipped, set down his glass, and folded his arms, his gaze steady. "Friendship," he repeated firmly. "You know I can't violate my patient-physical therapist code of ethics, however charmingly you bat your eyelids."

"Can't or shouldn't?"

"Shouldn't… *and* can't." Alec's dimples reappeared. "I admire the persistence, though."

Tyler took it as a compliment and grinned. "Thanks. We're stubborn little assholes, aren't we?"

"You can say that again." Alec laughed, but he was relaxing slightly, having said his piece.

Tyler nodded slowly. "I get it. You don't want to get in trouble, and I don't, either. I mean… professionally, I'm in a kind of tight place." When Alec raised his eyebrows, he sighed. "I'm closeted at work, technically. There's never been a big-name out gay driver. Ever. It's one of the few sports where we're still invisible."

Alec nodded. "And I told myself I wouldn't date anyone closeted. Or, you know, pick up."

"I wouldn't say I'm closeted, though." Tyler shook his head. "I'm pretty damn out in the rest of my life, so I've been waiting for years for it to bite me in the ass." Why the hell was he saying this? He'd only just sat down.

Alec didn't push him, though. He just nodded slightly. "I get it. It must be hard. I take it you're not seeing anyone, then."

Tyler sighed and shook his head slightly.

"But… you'd like to? In the future?"

He's getting straight to the point. I like it. Tyler wasn't used to running into guys who didn't dance in circles, afraid to say what they meant or ask questions. "I don't know," he admitted. "I'm really good at fucking. I'm a hopeless flirt. I'm always on the road. Guys tend to have problems with one of those things."

"Why is the first one a problem?" Alec asked, laughing.

"It's what I'm *not* good at," Tyler said. He fidgeted, sipping a few times as he tried to figure out how to say it without making Alec run the other way. "You know. Feelings."

"The relationship stuff," Alec said.

"Yeah. That."

Alec nodded, those sexy lips pursing around the rim of his glass as he drank. When he set his glass down, he answered, "So you're putting your career on the line to… pick up guys?"

"Despite appearances, I'm pretty careful," Tyler said. He laughed. "You just flagged up my gaydar."

Alec frowned. "Did I? Shit."

Tyler realized he hadn't returned the questions, and he wanted to know why Alec had reacted that way. "You're not out?"

"No. My line of work…"

Coming from the background he did, Tyler instantly understood. As much as fellow drivers would get uncomfortable around a gay guy changing an engine next to them, they'd be worse having one feel them up. "Yeah. I get it," he quickly assured Alec.

"But you still find it's worth the… the risk?" Alec asked slowly.

"Don't you? I mean, I don't want to assume every gay guy in the world hooks up as much as me…" Tyler snorted.

Alec chuckled. "I try. But most of the guys I know are former patients, so they're all… well…"

Closeted, like me. Tyler sighed and nodded slightly. "Fuck all that bullshit," he murmured, holding his glass up.

Alec clinked it to toast the sentiment and smiled. "I was reading up on you. You've got a name for yourself."

Tyler wasn't going to pass up the opportunity to brag. "Oh, yeah. Why?"

"Well…" Alec hummed, propping his chin on his fist. "It's not often I run into guys who have maybe even more to lose than me. So why take the risk on me?"

Tyler had a few smooth lines to choose from: he could compliment Alec for being hot, or say he was just following instinct.

But what was true, really?

"You're the first guy who hasn't just wanted to come back to my place and screw when I gave them the Ty grin."

Alec's eyebrows shot up. "The Ty grin?"

That did sound a little egotistic, Tyler had to admit, but it wasn't out of character for him. Largely because he didn't pick up women left, right, and center, he'd been typecast as a southern gentleman in the driving world. Polite and chivalrous, but confident in who he was and what he was capable of doing. Like winning.

"It's part of my brand." Tyler flashed that grin. "Charms the panties off the ladies."

Alec laughed. "That's unfortunate."

Tyler burst out laughing, his hand instinctively pressing to his rib to make it hurt less. "Right? It works on men, too, though."

Alec licked his lips and sipped quickly, a blush rising to his cheeks again as he looked down at the table.

Now was a good time to press him. "Is it working on you?" Tyler asked. "Enough to get you to bend the rules a bit?" He dialed up the charm and propped his chin on his fist.

"Maybe," Alec murmured, his eyes still on his beer. "If we did screw, it can't get out. Ever."

"I'm asking *you*, you're not picking me up."

Alec sighed patiently as he looked up at him. "That doesn't matter to licensing boards. Especially if you're a guy. They would care less if you were a woman."

"Fuckers," Tyler muttered under his breath. "Well, you're right. I have more to lose than you. And I trust you." He wasn't sure why, but Alec had a hell of a trustworthy face.

Alec nodded slightly, his gaze finally rising to meet Tyler's. "I told myself not to fuck on first dates anymore."

Is he *looking for a relationship first?* Tyler looked back, not daring to break the gaze. "But?"

"Take me on a date," Alec told him, tipping his chin up in a challenge. "And give me a chance to decide how stupid I want to be."

"It's a date." Tyler glanced around, then reached over the table to brush his fingers along the back of Alec's hand. He straightened up again and winked. "I'll give you a chance. We have weeks of treatment ahead, right?"

"Oh, you're a handful."

"Two, actually. Unless you have real big hands."

Alec's cheeks turned bright red, and he choked on his beer.

Tyler grinned wickedly. "Sorry."

"Liar."

"Yeah. Not sorry. You're cute when you blush," Tyler told Alec. He swigged his beer, smirking when Alec tried to drown himself in his beer.

Maybe this was a longer game than he'd thought, but it was gonna be worth it. With weeks of frustration lying ahead of him, Alec could be the perfect distraction.

Josh and the other guys will flip their shit when I tell them I've seen the same guy more than once. It was almost worth it for that alone.

That was decided, then. Now that he had Alec's tacit permission to date him and try to get into his pants before treatment was over, Tyler was going to have fun with it.

CHAPTER
Six

ALEC

"Oh, for fuck's sake."

Alec had been trying to make scrambled eggs while lost in thought, and he'd just cracked an egg directly into the frying pan. It sizzled before he could even think about scrambling it. Sunny-side-up eggs for breakfast, then.

They hadn't even shared a good night kiss, but Alec was still daydreaming about last night. They'd stayed at the bar until almost closing time, talking about anything and everything. Tyler had apparently taken the talk as permission to keep flirting with him all damn night long.

Once again, a guy batted his lashes at him and Alec fell over himself to say yes to whatever he proposed.

It was so fucking hard to resist Tyler's grin, even if it was deliberately calculated to charm. Tyler definitely used it while they were interviewing him on TV, asking if there were any girlfriends in the picture.

Alec sighed, peeking at the underside of the egg as it bubbled gently in the pan. Everything about this seemed like a bad idea: they both had careers to lose.

By rights, they should only be friends. Hell, according to his code of ethics, even that much was iffy. He could make *some* excuses: it wasn't unheard-of for physical therapists who worked with teams to be invited to team social events. One-on-one, though?

Alec rested the spatula on the side of the pan and folded his arms as he paced back and forth.

"I don't need to fuck every hot guy who walks into my life. Not even if he's smart and interesting and sweet..."

Tyler came off as full of himself when he was flirting, but when he actually talked, he was engaging. He'd taken an interest in Alec's opinions, not just his career or his ass.

He was charming, sexy, strong, and though he claimed he was only a gentleman for the cameras, he was considerate—he'd thanked the glass collectors.

"Oh, hell, no."

Alec was *not* considering Tyler as dating material. No way. Tyler had made it clear he didn't do that. Alec couldn't even risk a sexual relationship with a current patient. An emotional relationship? The risk there was far deeper than professional.

It was way too easy to get attached. And sooner or later, reality had to come crashing back down... didn't it?

A slight scorching smell brought him rushing back to the pan to dump the cooked egg onto his toast.

Just as Alec set his plate on the table and reached for his phone, it danced across the surface, vibrating with an incoming call.

It was Tyler. As much as he might deny his feelings, he couldn't deny the way his heart fluttered when he saw the name on his display.

"Hey," Alec answered once he brought the phone to his

ear. He tried to remind himself that Ty was just a friend. No need to be nervous. "How's it going?"

"Hi." Tyler's voice sent butterflies through him, try as he might to stay calm. "I'm real good. Just wanted to say thanks for last night. I had a great time."

"Really?" Alec was so caught off-guard he hardly knew what to say. His cheeks burned, but it wasn't unpleasant. Had a guy ever called him after a date to say thank you? "Um. I mean. I-I did, too."

"Phew. I was getting worried for a second," Tyler said and snorted with laughter. "*Really, man? Because I was bored the whole night.*"

"No, no," Alec laughed. "I wasn't. I was, uh, just thinking about it over breakfast."

"Oh, shit. Did I interrupt you? Sorry."

"No, it's okay." Alec was suddenly too nervous to eat, which was a whole new one for him.

"I guess you have weekends off?" Tyler followed up.

Oh my God. Is he gonna ask me out again?

"Yeah." Alec didn't bother to ask about Ty's schedule and reemphasize the importance of rest. "Just errands, and… you know. Hanging out. At home. God, that makes me sound like a loser."

"No. You aren't," Tyler said, and the ever-present confidence in his voice filled Alec with warm appreciation.

"You don't need to be gentle."

Ty's voice dropped to a rough growl. "I'll remember that."

Alec tried to answer, but his voice just cracked for a second. He cleared his throat, then laughed. "Yeah." Fuck. He was starting to get hard again. How the fuck did Ty turn him on with a couple of words?

"And," Ty added, his voice softer, "I don't bullshit people. I like you. If I didn't, you'd know that, too."

Alec paused. "Oh." It fit with what he'd figured out already about Tyler—direct and no-nonsense. "As a friend?"

"Not just a friend, but if that's what you want, yeah."

"I could come over this weekend." *Oh, for fuck's sake.* Alec was impatient with himself the moment he heard the words leave his mouth, but not enough so to take it back. He *did* want Tyler, regulations be damned.

Maybe they could get this sexual chemistry out of the way with a good fuck, then focus on Tyler's recovery like they should be doing.

"I'm staying with a friend, but I'll come to your place. Text me your address," Tyler told him. He chuckled gently. "Does this mean you've thought about it?"

"Yeah, but I seem to be in *impulsive decision* mode," Alec admitted.

"I can come over now, if that helps."

Alec opened his mouth to tell Tyler to wait, but… why? If he was gonna do this, he might as well get it out of the way with now instead of worrying about it all afternoon.

Instead, Alec licked his lips. "Okay."

"Perfect." Tyler chuckled. "As soon as you text me your address. See you in a few."

"Will do in a sec. See you," Alec murmured.

Alec's hand shook as he typed his address into the text message window, then set his phone on the counter and covered his face for a few moments.

The phone went off, and he barely dared glance down at it. When he finally steeled his courage, the message just said, *On my way. Gimme 20.*

Oh, fuck. That was barely enough time to eat breakfast, tidy the place, and change into something sexy.

Twenty minutes and he'd get this out of his system. And *then* he'd ask the next guy to take him on a date first.

The doorbell rang, and Alec just about flew to the door to answer.

He tried to pat his hair into place and wait a second behind the door before opening it, but he didn't last long. Hands trembling with anticipation, he unlocked the door.

Tyler was every inch as sexy filling up his doorway as he had been in the bar last night, and before that, on his examination table—*no, don't do that,* he tried to tell his brain to be professional. It was in vain, though. His brain was taking off with ideas.

Just to finish Alec off, Ty greeted him with that slow, sweet smile that flashed his perfect, white teeth. "Hey, sexy."

How the hell did he have such good teeth? Hadn't steering wheels taken out any of them? For that matter, how was he so fucking hot that just being fixed with his stare made heat flush through Alec from head to toe?

"Hi," Alec answered, reading the charged atmosphere between them. They weren't gonna make it another ten seconds without kissing. Maybe it was just the allure of the forbidden, but the charge between them was even thicker than before.

He pushed the door closed and leaned against it.

Tyler pivoted to keep facing him as he did so, and then stepped close, his hand resting along the side of Alec's face. "Do you want to kiss me?"

"Please." Alec's voice came out in a whisper at the sensation of those gentle fingers against his stubble.

And then, at last, Tyler's lips were against his.

They felt perfect. In a way Alec couldn't describe, this felt like exactly the right thing right now. He felt complete, whole, contented for just a few moments.

Maybe because the kiss was slow and unhurried, even though they were both in a hurry—he could feel Tyler getting hard against his thigh as soon as Tyler stepped close enough that they brushed together.

Maybe because Tyler's eyes, half-lidded, seemed to see *him*. Tyler was watching his reactions like he wanted him to feel good.

Maybe because he liked the guy. He knew him less than any of his patients—they'd only just met, for God's sake—but Tyler didn't seem to have layers, despite being closeted. He was simple and direct and straightforward.

What Tyler wanted, he took. And Tyler wanted Alec. And Alec wanted to be taken.

He moaned, his lips parting at the idea of that hard cock rubbing between his thighs, pressing into him. Tyler was small and compact, like most race car drivers, but he was still strong as hell—and broader than Alec. He could easily manhandle Alec, just like he was pressing him up against the door right now.

Whatever token resistance he'd put up at first melted when Tyler looked at him like he thought Alec was worth chasing. Alec couldn't be annoyed at himself for giving in when Tyler was there, the sexual tension making his head spin and knees weaken.

Their lips were hot and wet now, each of them breathing in quick, sharp gasps between kisses. They couldn't seem to stop now, their hands wandering up each other's backs, down their sides, across their asses.

Tyler was squeezing his ass, and it felt so fucking *good*.

Alec whimpered and closed his eyes. "I want you," he let himself whisper, but he was also feeling strangely shy.

Vulnerable.

Tyler knew almost nothing about him—where he'd grown up, what he did for a living, what he thought of the government, even the standard small talk you'd make on a first date at a bar. But Tyler seemed to care about *him*. He'd paid attention, asked questions, and hell, he'd backed off when Alec told him he needed time to think about this.

Why the hell was he so vulnerable around him?

Alec didn't have time to think about it. Tyler was pressing up against him, and Alec could feel him shift his weight off his bad leg.

One more reminder that this was a bad idea. Forbidden. Wrong. That he shouldn't want this—want Ty.

But he did.

"Come on," he whispered, grabbing Tyler and towing him down the hall to the living room.

His brain was shutting down. All he cared about now was pleasure—his and Tyler's. Making them both feel good. Getting this out of their systems so maybe he could *finally* look at Ty and not picture him naked.

He pushed Tyler down onto the couch and straddled him, kissing him hard.

Tyler's hands slid up under his tight t-shirt, nails raking the skin and sending sparks of maddening desire through him. He ground against Tyler's lap, stifling the gasp when their hard cocks made contact and rubbed, even through layers of fabric.

"Naked," Tyler demanded in a whisper. "Now."

Alec raised a brow at that attitude, but he grinned. He couldn't pretend he didn't like that Tyler knew exactly what he wanted. "Yes, sir." He shrugged his shirt off as soon as Tyler gave him enough space, then yanked off Tyler's button-up.

Their jeans came off next, and he was as gentle as he knew how to be, considering Tyler's injuries.

God, he was bruised up. The mottled, dark patches of skin made him wince and hesitate. But Tyler grabbed his chin and pulled him in for another hard kiss, clearly trying to distract him—and maybe himself.

"God, you're too hot for your own good. I want you," Tyler whispered. Hah. As if Alec hadn't already seen his hard cock pressed up against his stomach, telling him the exact same thing.

Alec tried to slow down enough to appreciate all the sensations, but Tyler was playing him like a fiddle. Light touches to his back and sides reminded him of the urgency in his groin. When Ty pulled his hips close enough that their hard shafts rubbed together, Alec groaned.

He wanted to suck that hard, thick shaft and get a look up close, but Tyler was still kissing him, sucking his lower lip slowly and running his tongue along it.

Goddamn, Tyler was a good kisser. Alec squirmed on Tyler's lap, his own cock sliding along Tyler's stomach and those gorgeous abs.

When Tyler finally let him have breath, he whispered, "I want you to ride me. If you can handle me."

Alec raised his brow and tipped his chin up, meeting Tyler's gaze defiantly. "I can handle you." As big as Tyler was, Alec was confident about that much.

He hadn't fucked this many guys without learning to predict how goddamn good a cock would feel from one look at it. Tyler was big, but not painfully so. His cock had the well-proportioned, thick, straight shaft that made for his absolute favorite kind of dick.

"I can deep-throat you, too," Alec casually added.

Tyler's lips parted in surprise, and then his face lit up. "Yeah?"

Alec grinned and scooted off the couch to kneel between Tyler's legs without another word. He preferred to show, not tell.

"Oh, fuck," Tyler moaned as Alec wrapped his lips around Ty's rounded head, running his hand experimentally down the cock to the base.

Alec sucked his cheeks in and slowly took in an inch at a time, relishing the fresh, clean scent of soap mixed with the thick taste of precum sliding across the back of his tongue.

Fuck. He should have gotten a condom out. He'd gotten so damn hungry for it that he hadn't even thought twice about it. Like Tyler was the oxygen he needed so badly he couldn't think straight.

Suddenly, he couldn't remember a hookup he'd had in the last year that compared to this. Most of them were almost incidental—hot guy propositioned, he said yes, they did the job.

But now? Alec was eager to please, his gaze flickering up to Tyler's face whenever he could look up that far to watch his expressions. Tyler's cock bumped the back of Alec's throat and he swallowed instinctively, then relaxed, his hand teasing the inside of Tyler's thigh.

He felt a need that ran so deep he didn't quite understand it yet.

For intimacy? For someone to take as big a risk on him as he took on them? Wasn't that just a desire for vulnerability?

For more than empty sex?

Oh, God. I don't want this to be it between us. Aren't I supposed to at least wait until we've hooked up before I decide that?

"You're so sexy," Tyler whispered, his hand running gently through Alec's hair. He gripped his shoulders and squeezed, massaging lightly. "Your mouth is fucking talented."

Sex. It's just sex. Alec pulled himself back to the moment and pulled his mouth slowly off Tyler, then bobbed his head quickly a few more times, getting into a quick rhythm before he pulled back and strode for the bedroom.

When he came back with lube, Tyler had arranged the pillows behind himself, his legs spread, one hand around his glistening, thick cock.

God, what a sight.

"Ready to climb on, gorgeous?" Tyler grinned, his hand jerking his cock slowly. "Gimme a couple weeks and I'll show you speed."

Is that an offer for more? No. It's just sexy talk, he reminded himself. Goddamn, he had to get it together. This was no different from any other no-strings-attached hookup.

"I can go for miles," Alec assured Tyler with an equally cocky grin back at him, giving him a taste of his own medicine.

Tyler's eyes widened, and he licked his lips. Apparently, he liked the attitude. "Fuck, yeah. Show me what you can do, baby."

Alec grinned as he straddled Tyler again, sliding wet fingers into himself. "I'm gonna need this first," he whispered.

"Take your time." Once he'd rolled the condom on, Tyler's hand slid down Alec's back to rest gently on his wrist. "That's so damn hot."

Alec's fingers were nowhere near as thick and satisfying as he wanted right now. He slid them out at last and gripped Tyler's cock, then pressed it against himself and slowly sank down.

The first few seconds were always the strangest, and now was no exception as his body adjusted to having the full thickness of Tyler inside him. All thoughts of taking it carefully went out the window, though, when he slid down at just the right angle to rub his prostate with Tyler's cock.

Sparks of pleasure flew through him, electric tingles chilling his spine and warming his cheeks. "Yes," Alec panted under his breath, thrusting again—a little harder.

He gripped Tyler's shoulders to keep himself steady and upright, his muscles quickly adjusting to the demand as he rose and sank.

"God, you're hot," Tyler groaned. "You feel so good. Wish I could show you how good."

Alec smiled cheekily at him. "Just keep telling me, then."

"Oh, you like hearing me talk dirty? I like having my cock in you," Tyler murmured, his hands running up Alec's sides— never as high as his cheeks, though. His movement was clearly still limited, however much he played it off as no big deal.

It made Alec move with precision and caution, even though the lust running through his veins made him want to fuck Tyler with wild abandon.

"I like seeing you fuck yourself on me, hard and fast. Watching your cock twitch when you hit just the right spot."

If his cheeks hadn't already been hot from exertion, they

would have burned at the words. He was so turned on he could hardly find the words to answer Tyler—he just stared at him, his movements faltering for a moment before he thrust himself down on his lap again, faster.

If this was a bad idea, he was going to make the most of every second of it.

More to the point, he was going to enjoy feeling like he was worth the risk. Maybe this was a one-time deal—it almost certainly was, given their situation—but it was the hottest sex he'd had in living memory.

He wasn't sure what about the encounter was so scorching hot, besides the fact he was playing with fire. Was it because Tyler ran his hand gently up Alec's back, as if he were fighting himself to keep from taking over? The way Tyler looked at him instead of closing his eyes or looking away? Or, just maybe, did Tyler feel the same spark of connection that seemed to jolt between them without any effort?

It was so damn nice not to have to fake pleasure. For once, Alec had to try to keep himself in check instead. He was not going to come before he'd even been riding Tyler for five minutes. He had *some* pride, after all.

"Fuck," Tyler whispered. He was still touching Alec's back lightly, licking his lips as he looked him up and down. "You're every bit as hot as I'd hoped. Goddamn. Where have you been hiding my whole life?"

Alec grinned and tossed his head. "Around."

"Not around me, or I would've noticed." Tyler groaned, his nails digging into Alec's hip. "I like the way your hips move when you walk."

"Someone's been eyeing my ass in the office," Alec laughed.

"Damn straight. Well, not at all straight." Tyler smirked, then pulled him in gently to kiss him. He murmured against his lips, "As gay as it's possible to get without actually pulling down your pants and bending you over your own exam table."

Alec whimpered against Tyler's mouth, his lips parting. Tyler eagerly seized his chance to bite Alec's lower lip, sucking it until Alec squirmed on his cock, his motions becoming less fluid.

"Now you're gonna think about it, too," Tyler whispered. "A load shared…"

"Is a sticky mess for both of us," Alec snorted. "Thanks, man." Already, he was seeing how damn hard it was going to be to focus when Tyler next saw him. And his motions sped up as he shifted to let his hips and gravity do the hard work.

Thrust after thrust, he enveloped Alec deep within, taking his whole cock without hesitation now. All that escaped were moans and whimpers.

"That's it, baby," Tyler gasped. "Oh, God. I'm gonna come soon. Come for me, hon. Let me see you lose it. I wanna watch you jerk yourself off."

Alec shoved a hand between them to grip his own pulsating length, stroking himself hard and fast as he fucked Tyler, taking him as deep as he could.

"Yes!" Alec cried when it hit him—faster and harder than usual. He had almost no warning, just the overwhelming need for release, and Tyler whispering encouragement in his ear about how fucking sexy he found it to watch him come.

His body pressed as hard against Tyler's as he dared, which was gentle, but still enough that his passion spilled across both of them. And Tyler's hands closed around his hips as he thrust up a few more times, then grunted, his head rolling back.

Alec grinned as he watched Tyler finish, staying perfectly in place to let Tyler join him in the orgasmic bliss that made his limbs heavy and his heart light.

"Oh, fuck," Tyler finally panted when he started to soften and collapsed again. A hand went to his ribs.

Alec covered Tyler's hand with his own. "Is it hurting? A new kind of pain?"

Tyler's lips twitched into a smile as he opened his eyes again, meeting Alec's gaze and shaking his head. "No, darling. But thank you. That's… it's nice that you care."

"Of course I do." Alec snorted and shook his head. "I am your medical professional. Or I'm supposed to be." Without a doubt, this was the stupidest thing he'd done—and the hottest. He knew he *should* regret it, but he didn't. Not for a second.

Tyler pulled his hand away so that Alec's hand rested against his ribs, and he covered Alec's hand with his own. "I'm really glad you said yes."

"Me, too," Alec admitted, and then he found himself staring at Tyler's bruised chest, not quite able to meet his gaze. The stillness between them seemed to draw to a close, and the *shoulds* and *shouldn't*s rushed in to take its place.

Tyler cleared his throat. "I should, um… get cleaned up and call a cab."

"I—I guess so." Alec gave Tyler a hand sitting up straight, then standing up. It was only when they were in the bathroom and he was helping Tyler pull his shirt on again that it hit him: taking care of Tyler wasn't strictly professional. He was concerned about him as more than his physical therapist.

He cared about all his patients, sure. He looked after them. But he'd never slipped up and fucked any of them before while they were still his patients—even the ones who'd hit on him so hard his head spun.

Something about Tyler made him want to say yes to him, even when his ideas were dumb. Maybe it was the puppy eyes and proper manners. Alec was gonna have to watch out for himself. This guy was trouble.

It was only after Alec saw Tyler out to a cab that he realized he couldn't seem to shake the goofy grin.

He's trouble, but I like trouble. Way more than is good for me.

CHAPTER
Seven

TYLER

"Can I make breakfast, at least? Or are you tying me to the bed?"

Josh poked his head in the doorway of Tyler's room and grinned at him. "If only you'd offered me that option years ago."

Tyler was trying to sit up, but man, he'd never known how weak his core muscles were. Considering the strength and endurance it took to hold himself properly in a race car seat, that was saying something.

"You lie there," Josh told him firmly, waving a hand. "Don't be an asshole."

"You're being an asshole," Tyler muttered back, childishly.

"Yep. In fact, I am the biggest asshole."

"I heard that from Grindr. Oh, wait. You said *am*, not *have*."

Josh flipped him off. "I'll bring you breakfast in a minute. Are you actually gonna stay in bed today instead of flirting your way around town?"

"We'll see." Tyler smirked and waited until Josh was out

of earshot before he crunched his way upright and slowly climbed out of bed.

He got dressed as quietly as he could, but even so, Josh yelled, "I can hear you moving around in there."

"Dammit." Tyler laughed to himself at Josh's super-hearing. "I'm fine," he called back. Once he had sweatpants and a loose t-shirt on, he shuffled his way to the kitchen to join Josh and put the coffee on.

Josh scowled at him as he flipped the bacon. "You're worse about resting than I am." That was saying something—Tyler rarely saw Josh take a day off, if ever. He never seemed to get sick, or if he did, he sneakily chugged Dayquil and kept on ticking.

"Yeah. But that's it, isn't it?" Tyler gingerly lowered himself onto one of the stools at the breakfast bar and folded his arms on top of it. It didn't really matter how he sat or whether or not he took his painkillers—everything ached. The injuries had sunk into his very bones and spread around his whole body.

He'd been injured pretty badly before: broken limbs here and there, plenty of strains and sprains, and the occasional whiplash. This was the worst accident so far, though. And he wasn't eighteen anymore. He might only be reluctantly admitting and admitted to his late twenties now, but injury recovery slowed year after year. If he managed to keep his career that long, he hoped the league kept improving its safety by the time he was pushing forty.

Josh waggled his spatula in front of Tyler's face to get his attention. "What's it?"

"Oh." The meds made Tyler feel spaced-out, and the concentration it took to maintain conversation was hard to overestimate. He kept forgetting how forgetful he was. "I mean, everyone around here is working. Even the honey-mooners are going out trail riding."

"There's the coffee. Grab the sugar." Josh might have sounded unsympathetic if Tyler didn't know him so well.

Tyler swung himself down from the stool and reached up to the cupboard above the coffee maker. Then he winced and stopped when his rib twanged, almost doubling over for breath.

"See?" Josh came up behind him. For once, the hand on his shoulder was gentle, even if his tone wasn't. "You can't do shit. Don't get yourself even more screwed up. Take the time to heal right." He grabbed the sugar jar from the cupboard, and Tyler had never been more jealous of anyone being able to reach as high as their face.

Thank God he had low-maintenance hair. He laughed to himself. As he did so, pressing a hand to his ribs came instinctively, before he'd even thought about it. Another little habit to cope with the pain, making it bearable to laugh. "Fine," he muttered. "Asshole."

"Dick. We're the perfect pair."

He laughed again and winced harder this time. "Ow."

"Here's breakfast." Josh slid a plate across the counter and came to join him. Tyler hated noticing Josh moving carefully around him, because it was a reminder of how breakable he must look right now.

"Thanks, man. For..." Tyler waved around.

"Duh," Josh told him and rolled his eyes. "Not like you were going home in this state."

Staying with Josh hadn't even been a question, no matter how stubborn he was. Tyler knew damn well couldn't have gotten up the stairs to his little apartment downtown, not that he lived there for more than a couple days at a time during the racing season.

It reminded him of how Roman, another good friend, had wound up falling in love—by hosting Oscar, an injured dancer who'd needed a place to stay that was on the ground floor.

He snorted at the idea of falling for Josh.

"What?"

"It's like Roman and Oscar, but I don't even get the benefits."

Josh eyed him as they both wolfed down breakfast with the appetites of racehorses. "You're doing fine getting your own benefits. I swear to God, you'd have to be in a coma to avoid finding the hottest nurse around and doing him."

The mention of himself in a compromising position with a healthcare professional made Tyler flinch. He covered it up by shifting position and wincing, then laughed. *I'm sure Alec was just being overly careful, but still... if he doesn't want to give it away, I gotta be more careful.* "Yeah? Even so, it worked for Sleeping Beauty, right?"

"The Disney version or the original?"

"There's an original?"

"Dude." Josh wrinkled his nose as he cleaned his plate. "Yeah. It's a lot grosser. And you're not that beautiful when you sleep."

Tyler laughed richly, startled into it so quickly that he didn't have time to grab his chest first. His ribs complained. "Ow. God. You're gonna be out of the house for a good long time today, right?"

Josh grinned. "Yeah, yeah. I'll be out of your hair soon, Briar Rose."

"Don't make me test the other arm," Tyler warned, pushing his plate back.

"See? There's the thorns." Josh dodged Tyler's half-hearted swing and winked as he got up to gather their plates and clean up. It made Tyler feel shitty that he couldn't even help with that yet. "Fine, fine. I'm gone. Don't miss me too much. Don't forget, we're going out with the guys tonight, too."

"I'll send my love letters by paper airplane." Tyler rolled his eyes at Josh and pushed himself away from the counter to limp over to the sofa. He was gonna be stuck sitting around a lot over the next couple weeks, but at least he had a lot to do to distract him today.

After lunch, he had to call a couple people and update them on the recovery, and go downtown for a long-overdue bank appointment.

But first, he had an interview at the top of the hour. A long-time car blogger with a wry sense of humor, Bobby was always good for a laugh. Tyler was gonna have to keep a pillow on his chest all day.

Just as he thought that, Tyler's phone timer went off, reminding him to breathe. The risk of pneumonia compelled him to do his hourly deep breathing, even if he cursed at the stupid fucking thing for chiming so damn often throughout these boring days.

As soon as he was done and back to comfortably shallow breaths, Tyler dialed Bobby's number and settled himself on the couch.

"Hey, man." Bobby sounded perky as ever. He'd always come across as a kind of practical joker, much like Tyler in his own group of friends. "Thanks for calling in. I'm just getting the recording equipment set up. How's it going?"

"Pretty shitty right now," Tyler told him with a chuckle. "But getting there."

"Back on the farm, huh?"

Tyler didn't even ask how he'd heard. He was getting used to word spreading before he knew about it. "Yeah. My buddy's not even putting the sugar on the top shelf… yet."

"Good," Bobby laughed. "Getting to see your other friends? Say, uh, that… Deen, isn't it? The bi rock star? He's one of your buddies, isn't he?"

The inclusion of Deen's sexuality made Tyler take pause. Bobby had never seemed like the kind of guy who'd dig around for a dirty scoop, but the fucked-up thing about his situation was how much it made him question the motives of everyone around him. "Yeah," he said. "Why?"

"Well, uh… he's engaged to that guy you know, isn't he? And you're going to stay with a single guy on a farm…"

"If you're asking something, spit it out." Tyler's voice was flatter than he'd meant it to be.

"No," Bobby said firmly. "I don't give a shit. It's not what my readers care about, anyway. But you should know, tongues are wagging. I don't talk a lot to that sphere of the car world, but I've… heard stuff."

"The usual rumor mill, then," Tyler said dryly. "Like spinning out and nearly dying ain't enough of a scoop for them."

"They won't be happy 'til they know way more than it's their business knowing," Bobby said and sighed. "Just about ready, sorry. Been having trouble with the system lately. I swear to God this ain't recorded, either."

"Yeah. I trust you," Tyler said simply. It *had* occurred to him, and he'd felt briefly bad thinking it. "Thanks for the heads-up."

"Least I can do. I can't say a lot about them, you know…

tell them to fuck off and mind their own business in public. They get so much traffic, so many hits…"

"Yeah. I get it. Nobody wants to stick their neck out," Tyler said, reaching up to rub his chin before he winced. That was reaching little higher than was comfortable.

"That's for damn sure." Bobby cleared his throat. "Right. Okay, this thing seems to be working now. Do you wanna get started?"

Tyler tried to drag his mind off the conversation, and stop himself from wondering who the hell was digging around his life. "I'm ready when you are."

If something came out right when he was injured and useless to his current team… well… it was gonna be a hell of a ride. Just when his life seemed to be slowing to an unbearable crawl, it had gone from zero to sixty in a totally different area.

Typical.

THE LAST THING ALEC EXPECTED WAS A TEXT MESSAGE FROM Tyler, a couple minutes after the office closed.

Wanna go for a drink?

Alec eyed the message for a minute. Tyler really ought to be on painkillers still, which meant he was either putting himself in unnecessary medical danger or unnecessary pain if he meant a *drink* drink.

Plus, alcohol could make the boundaries between them… well… blurrier than they'd already been. The memory made his cheeks burn with pleasure, though.

Coffee? Alec chose to answer, biting his thumbnail as he walked to his car, phone clutched tightly in his hand. It wouldn't be a bad idea to meet up again anyway, and go over the finer details of their relationship.

He'd slipped up once already—he couldn't keep it up.

His phone vibrated with Tyler's response: *Sure. I'm already downtown. Tell me when & where ;)*

God, the wink was almost too much. Alec sighed to himself, trying to shelve his feelings for the guy. He really had to get his shit together. *I'm around the corner from Star-bucks. Meet there in 15?* He pocketed his car keys again. May as well stay parked here and walk to the coffee shop if he was heading straight there.

Uh... that's where I am. Are you spying on me? Was I sexy this morning?

Alec couldn't resist a laugh, his cheeks flushing with heat as he altered his course for the coffee shop.

He was still disappointed in himself for promising himself he wouldn't fuck Tyler, and immediately breaking that promise. The rules were there for a reason. A doctor-patient relationship could never have the same power dynamic as a healthy sexual relationship, and...

Oh, man. There was Tyler, sitting in the window, looking casually gorgeous—the kind of guy Alec would crane his neck back to check out a second or third time, if he'd just been walking down the street.

And he was about to have coffee with him.

Never mind the mistakes he'd already made... how the fuck was he going to keep it in his pants from now on?

"That wasn't fifteen minutes at all," Tyler greeted with a grin as he walked in. The slightly cocky, yet sexy self-assurance of the way he held himself even when injured... it was easy to forget until he walked into the same space as Tyler again and got knocked off his feet again.

Fucking fuck. It was easy to theorize about the best way to keep his distance, but there was something that pulled Alec toward Tyler like they were magnets. Like Tyler was straight from the center of the earth, made of some trace element that was scattered through his cells.

Like Tyler was a piece of himself he hadn't even known he was missing.

Fuck. He craved touch sometimes like any guy, sure, but this wasn't just that. Everything from the way Tyler smiled to the nuances of his mind fascinated Alec, and he barely knew the guy. He'd never had this happen before.

"H-Hi," Alec managed, realizing he hadn't said a word yet. He braced himself on the back of the chair and tried to pull himself together again. "Fuck, sorry. Just got off work, my brain's fried."

Tyler winced sympathetically. "I bet. I'd have thought your hands would be the most tired, though."

"They're strong." Tyler's smirk said, *I know*, and Alec's cheeks flushed. "Uh, let me just…" Alec stuttered, trying not to let Tyler get those actual words out and embarrass him more. "Coffee. Want something?"

"Regular old latte would be great. Thanks," Tyler said, leaning forward to shove bills into his hand.

"No, I've got this." Alec tried to resist, but Tyler shook his head.

"I looked up the guidelines on professional relationships today, you know. Technically you're not allowed to buy me things." His eyes twinkled mischievously.

Fuck, he was a clever one. Alec glared, then cracked up as he took the bills. "*Now* you looked them up?"

"Yeah, yeah. Act first, ask permission later. Nothing would ever get done otherwise," Tyler said with a cheeky grin at him.

Alec was positive his blush was visible from space as he made his way for the counter. Hopefully the barista didn't feel it necessary to point it out. But she didn't, and just smiled at him as she asked his order.

"Um, two lattes. Medium. Thanks." Alec hadn't experienced the sensation of being tongue-tied like this before, either. Did it come with the kind of uncontrollable attraction to Tyler that he was trying not to trip into? Was he about to turn into a teen klutz, tripping into Tyler's arms?

That wouldn't go well, in Tyler's current state. He choked back the laugh at his own thought and paid for his coffee, then waited to bring the mugs back to the table.

It took all he had not to look at Tyler until he got back. If he looked over at him, he might just not look away again. Hell, the tips of his toes seemed to point toward Tyler whenever he was in the room—a prime sign of attraction.

Maybe lack of self-awareness wasn't the problem. He'd known perfectly well that he was going to make a mistake with this man from way too early in their relationship, even as brief as it had been so far. If only Alec *weren't* so goddamn self-aware. He could at least screw around with this guy without the professional guilt.

Alec swallowed the sigh and brought the coffee mugs back to the table. He couldn't avoid him any longer. "Here you go."

"Just what the doctor ordered." Tyler smirked and took his cup, his eyes fixed on Alec as Alec took a seat opposite him at the cozy table. "How was your day?"

"It was a day," Alec answered with a half-shrug. "Nothing much happened. I went for a run, but I've been thinking about trying a lower-impact sport. Mostly, I spent a lot of time thinking about… you know, a couple nights ago."

Tyler's grin was slow and meaningful. "Yeah? I did, too. In the shower."

Alec's cheeks were red as he looked around, but nobody else seemed to be listening in—or caring. He cleared his throat and looked back at Tyler. He was trying his hardest not to encourage it, but it sounded a lot like flirting was going on right now. "What about your day?"

"Meh." Tyler's smile wavered, which was unusual. "Just stuff."

Alec raised his eyebrows and resisted the urge to lean in. Something else was there, but pressuring Tyler wouldn't work, he didn't think. He just stayed patiently quiet until Tyler decided what to say about it.

Finally, Tyler sighed and gave in. "I had an interview with a blogger. He mentioned that someone's been sniffing around my personal life, looking for a scoop."

"A scoop that's there if they look hard enough?" Alec asked quietly, to avoid outing him in so many words.

Tyler nodded once.

Alec winced. "Fuck. Sorry." Then, he paused and tilted his head, his coffee mug halfway to his lips. "So the first thing you did was..."

"Call you up and meet in public? Yeah," Tyler laughed under his breath. He picked up his own mug and shrugged. "Never said I'm smart. I just drive cars."

Alec shook his head. "So, a scoop... do you mean, like, I should look out for paparazzi hiding in the bushes?"

"Nah." Tyler's chuckle was quiet, and he put a hand on his chest every time he laughed. Alec winced when he remembered the bruising across his chest, and the fractures that lay beneath. "I'm not that big. Yet. Which is why hanging out with guys isn't really a problem right now. Besides, normal guys do—I mean, you know..."

Alec winced but nodded. He knew what Tyler meant by *normal*: men who didn't have to hide selective pieces of their heart from the world at large.

Speaking of which, Tyler continued, "But I'm trying not to lose sponsorships."

"Ohhh." Alec had a vague idea of how the racing world worked, but he'd never bothered to look into it much. All his patients were concerned about losing them because of injuries and being sidelined, and it tended to be one of their main sources of income—that was all he'd needed to know.

"Yeah. Last season, my sponsor was actually really… gay-friendly," Tyler said, his voice uncharacteristically quiet. "It would've been okay. This year, I dunno. They've never said much publicly one way or another. But I lost last year's sponsor… to a teammate of the guy who nudged me."

"Oh, shit," Alec murmured, his brows drawing together in a frown. "That has to dial up the pressure."

"What kind of pressure?" Tyler asked.

Alec snorted. "To get back on the track, and to perform better, and… I don't know. Pull riskier moves than you might otherwise."

Tyler looked like he wanted to contest the point but couldn't. He finally sighed and nodded. "Yeah, I guess it does. I think there's something more going on behind the scenes, actually. Something with that team. Something they said before the race. But anyway, I ain't gonna prove it while I'm sitting around here doing nothing. How much longer, anyway?"

"Professional opinion?" When Tyler nodded, Alec blew out a sigh. "A week or two, minimum. Probably four weeks off in total. I'd prefer eight, but you'd never listen to me then."

Tyler winced. "So I'll miss a couple races. Goddamn."

"Sorry." Alec tried to change the subject subtly and get Tyler's mind off the enforced rest. "I always thought motorsports are riskier than some of the other sports I deal with, even without anything fishy going on."

He didn't want to ask too much—didn't want to know too much, if he were honest with himself. Which was silly. Not like the mafia owned car teams… or did they? He'd look that up later.

"It's not without its pit stops and pitfalls," Tyler said, his gaze on the surface of his coffee mug. "But it's worth it."

Alec pushed, "You're a smart guy, whatever you say. It's not just loud engines and sexy women, is it? There's something more that pushes every athlete. What do you get out of it?"

"Calling me smart?" Tyler wrinkled his nose at him. "Fuck off."

Alec just grinned at him. "Can't change my mind once I've made it up."

"Even with these long lashes?" Tyler winked.

"I'm immune," Alec said, flapping a hand. "Don't avoid the question."

Tyler laughed. "Fine, fine. I don't know. Can I say the money?"

Alec didn't believe that one, either. Tyler didn't act like a guy who had more money than common sense. He just raised his eyebrows.

Tyler looked strangely bashful for a moment, then glanced at the table to compose his thoughts. By the time he looked up, he looked ready to give an interview—passionate and certain of himself. "The rush and the adrenaline and all that macho stuff, obviously. But there's a thrill, too. That humans come together to make machines that can do *this*. That can get pushed to the limit for hours on end. And being the one human element in that machine, the thing that makes it all work, using physics… much like your job."

Alec just blinked at him. He sure as hell wasn't strapped into a boiling hot car for hours on end.

"You're using physics, right? But you're the human element manipulating it to do what you need. Anatomy is physics."

Alec understood. He pointed at Tyler and shook his head. "See? Smart." Tyler blew a raspberry, and Alec laughed. He hadn't seen anyone do that in so damn long. Maybe not since he was a kid, and… well, the sense of fun had gone away awfully fast.

As if reading Alec's mind again, Tyler swore. "Oh, shit on a stick. I gotta call Mom, I think," he said with a frown, glancing down at his phone. "I don't wanna ditch you early. I forgot. Sorry. The meds…"

Alec shook his head. "No, no. She'll wanna hear how you're getting on, I'm sure." *Most moms would,* he thought with a second of bitterness, but he pushed through it easily these days. Alec finished his coffee and stood up casually. "Besides, I've got errands. Are you fine to get home?"

"Yeah, my buddy's driving me home after I meet friends later. Thanks for the chat." Tyler offered him a smile as he stood to mirror Alec, and Alec instinctively mirrored the smile.

It was like they were in sync, which was a little weird, but also thrilling. "Thank you. Talk soon, yeah?" Alec kept it casual.

"Will do," Tyler promised, plugging earbuds with a built-in mic into his phone and placing it flat on the table. He glanced around, then turned his head to kiss Alec's cheek as he half-hugged him.

Oh, fuck. The warmth of his breath, and the smooth brush of his lips on Alec's skin made Alec's nerves tingle with excitement. It was all he could do to contain himself from giggling like a third-grade boy swapping cards on Valentine's Day.

"See you," Alec managed as he waved and left for his car with a lot more to think over than he'd had half an hour ago.

He's got a big and fast life, doesn't he? I could never keep up with all that. Hell, he's injured and he's doing interviews and calling his mom, and... all this stuff that isn't me.

Alec drew a deep breath and let it out.

It had to be just friendship. It was actually good that he'd seen Tyler briefly today, they'd talked more or less professionally, and he'd left to go home alone. The kiss... well... that could almost be written off as an accident, it had been so brief.

Maybe it would train his brain not to expect flirting and/or sex whenever they met.

Alec pressed his fingers to his cheek, his joyful smile cracking through the brisk facade. He felt light, and flirtatious, and *good*.

Yeah. Maybe pigs could fly.

CHAPTER

Nine

TYLER

God, Tyler would rather be anywhere but here.

Well, not *here*. It wasn't the bar's fault he had an unpleasant call to make. In this situation, rather—pacing in front of the bar, fingers curled tightly around his phone.

He kicked the curb, then winced as it sent a shockwave through his bad leg, too. Goddamn, he was useless right now.

"Alec won't let me get back to the track for at least this race. I might miss the next one, too." Tyler shook his head and hopped out of the way as a taxi driver caught his eye and slowed as if to pick him up. His gaze wandered to the doorway. Since he couldn't escape this conversation and join his friends yet, he headed for the bench outside instead.

"Right, right. You got banged up pretty bad." Of course Roger Marcson, the team owner, would already have heard as much. But Ty still had to make the call himself, and deal with the nerves that coursed through him.

"Yep. Hell of a crash. Couldn't have choreographed it if you'd tried." Tyler hesitated, not sure if he should mention that he was pretty sure it *had* been carefully planned.

Roger hummed. "Better not to push it if Alec says so. He's got a good reputation for not sugarcoating the truth. Want a second opinion?"

"No." Tyler spoke so fast he surprised himself twice over —at both the speed and content of his response.

What the hell? Of course he should take one. Cars could always be modified. But, in his heart, he trusted Alec's word —and he knew he wouldn't last the hours a race required. It wasn't just the final few laps of jostling for position. It was a long, slow grind. Fighting for your turf, lap after lap after damn lap. No high line ride outs. Definitely no single lines.

Summer was on its way, too. That meant 130º heat on a good day, 150º or more on a bad day, for hours on end. The blowers couldn't work magic. Racing kept a driver's mind off the heat, but if his body was already running on empty from the energy it took just to heal bad injuries like his?

He couldn't argue with Alec.

"No," Tyler clarified, blowing out a quick sigh. "I'll hope for the Bristol race. It's not off the table."

"Don't push yourself. I've been looking for a chance to try out Rory."

The mention of their spare driver gave Tyler a moment's pause. He was doing well, sure, but he couldn't afford to let Rory knock him off his pedestal. They could yank him from the car, and then... well, getting another chance wasn't a given.

It was a sensible decision—they had to run the car so they didn't lose the team points, but missing two races was going to fuck Tyler over as far as individual points. And he'd been doing so well, too.

It felt like a hand squeezing his heart, his chest was so tight. He swallowed hard and jerked his head to himself in a nod. "Yeah. Makes sense. Rory will do fine. He knows Kentucky well enough."

"Knows Bristol, too." Roger's tone was casual but pointed: he was measuring up his team. He didn't want Tyler to get lazy and assume he had all the time in the world to recover.

Tyler answered to acknowledge that he'd heard Roger's meaning. "He sure does." He made sure his voice was relaxed despite the frustration that knotted his guts. "I'll give you a call next week when I know more."

"Do that," Roger agreed. "Take care. Listen to Alec and get back on form for us."

Tyler would have rested his elbows on his knees and rubbed his chin if the move didn't make his ribcage protest. As it was, he had to stay sitting up, facing the world, like it or not. "Yes, sir."

When he hung up, Tyler took a minute to breathe and look around, watching passersby.

It was jarring to be stuck inside and kept from helping around the farm, but that call made him remember why he was doing it: speeding up his recovery by even a day or two meant he could get back to the track ASAP, and that was the most important thing in his life.

Or was it?

He glanced inside, to where his best friends—so close they called each other brothers—were no doubt joking around and chatting as usual. But a guy couldn't live life on friendship and fumes. More than the money, he needed his career to keep him on track and *going* somewhere.

Tyler knew himself. Without a purpose, he'd spin out of control. *Enough moping. Get your ass inside,* he told himself, hauling himself carefully to his feet and heading for the door.

"My round," he announced as he reached the table where

his buddies squeezed together in a rowdy group. Enough of them had boyfriends that their group had outgrown the booths now—they had to drag at least four chairs up to make those work now, when everyone turned up.

"That's what I like to hear," Josh approved. He reached out to slap Tyler's back.

Deen blocked his arm and smacked the back of Josh's head, which made everyone laugh. He'd been part of Nico's life for long enough that he was perfectly comfortable in their group now. "Don't break him even more."

"Need a hand carrying them back?" Nico offered.

"I'll help," Roman said with a wicked smirk that said he was planning something.

Oscar eyed him. "No, you won't. You stay here, trouble." He kissed Roman's cheek and stood up.

Nico, Oscar, and Tyler headed to the bar. The other two guys matched his pace without saying a word.

Tyler ordered a round of beers, then a couple shots of Southern Comfort.

"The call went that well, huh?" Nico looked sympathetic.

"Nothing I wasn't expecting," Tyler shrugged, wrapping his hand around one shot glass. He tipped his head back and downed it. Alcoholic heat blazed down his throat, sending a shock through his brain and waking him up in a hurry. "Phew," he gasped.

"The worst?" Oscar asked. Tyler had gathered he didn't know much about the sport, so he always tried to keep his explanations simple rather than exclude him.

"Nah." Tyler's voice was rough from the whisky burn until he cleared his throat. "They're running the car with the team's substitute driver. Smart for them."

"But risky for you," Nico said.

"Yep."

"I'm surprised you're not sneaking back out there anyway," Nico told him, lifting a brow and grinning. "That's your usual trick. Josh figured he'd have to post a watch on your door."

Tyler grimaced. "If only."

Nico was solemn for a moment, his gaze sharpening. He probably only realized now how serious it had been. "You're not having second thoughts about a career change?"

"Hell, no." Tyler snorted with laughter at how ridiculous the question seemed. He picked up the other shot and flung it into his throat. The burn felt good. Some kind of sensation, after days of being wrapped in wool. He curled his fingers around the edge of the counter and gasped to catch his breath.

"Just checking." Nico's hand rested on his shoulder for a moment. "It's just a temporary setback, then. You'll heal. You always do."

"Still pisses me off that Alec's right."

"Who?" Oscar frowned.

"The physical therapist. And he knows what he's doing. I can't argue it."

"You must hate that," Nico teased with a grin. "I've never known you not to argue something if you can help it."

Tyler flipped him off and handed over cash to the bartender, waving for him to keep the change, then grabbed four beers and headed for the table. Nico took four more, and Oscar the last two.

It was one of those rare days where everyone had made it out: Nico and Deen, Blane and Falcon, Roman and Oscar, and Dustin and Leo, plus Josh and himself.

"How'd it go?" Roman asked as soon as he was settled between him and Josh.

Tyler groaned. "Shitty. I gotta get back before Bristol. If I miss both of these…" he trailed off, staring through his beer bottle.

Roman shoved him lightly. "Hey. You'll be fine."

"You never know. You could meet a pretty farmhand," Deen said with a smirk. "Josh, you *do* hire the hot ones, right?"

"When I can help it," Josh said, grinning. "But I doubt we'll find our boy settling down anytime soon. Not if his weekend was anything to go by."

"Shut up," Tyler groaned, shaking a fist at his best friend. It was much less intimidating when he couldn't even lift it higher than his beer bottle, though.

Josh pretended to be scared anyway. "Help! The big, mean driver is gonna throttle me—haha, get it?"

"God," Tyler groaned. "Another week or two living with this font of shitty puns? Shoot me now."

"Hey. Only good things flow from me. If you know what I mean."

Tyler laughed despite himself, his hand pressing his rib automatically now. "Gross, dude. Besides," he said, looking back at Deen, "I'm not staying in town."

"Didn't stop me and Nico," Deen said, chuckling as he glanced sideways at his park ranger boyfriend.

Not a perfect example, Tyler thought. The bi rock star of their group had been on a break from touring when they'd met. He was back at it now, but he wasn't constantly on the road anymore. Hell, Nico had switched from full-time park ranger to another department so he could move out of the Smoky Mountains and live together with Deen in Knoxville.

Tyler, meanwhile, couldn't escape racing season or rearrange his career like they could. He just shook his head. "Besides, how do you know you've met the one? Everyone says *oh, you just know*." He gestured with the neck of his bottle between all the couples sitting around the table. "I haven't had that *you just know* feeling before. I doubt I'll start now."

The rest of them shared secretive smiles—standard *oh, wait until he feels it* shit. It might have pissed Tyler off if he cared about relationships at all.

"Watch out what you say. It's never when the timing is right." That was the newest member of their group, Leo, who had met Dustin at work. The two of them had sure as hell paid for the workplace relationship.

And they didn't even have a code of conduct in the way, or closets, or any of that shit. Every time Tyler wrote Alec off as a candidate for something longer-term, it seemed more sensible.

Didn't seem to stop Alec popping up in his head before anyone else, though. Weird. They'd barely known each other for a week now.

I'm gonna eat my hat if it is him. "Right, right," Tyler groaned and rolled his eyes to cover up his momentary worry, and the thrill of excitement that coursed through him at the very same moment.

Alec interested him. Something about him made Tyler want to get to know him more, even if Alec was trying to keep him at arms-length.

He was smart, funny, knowledgeable as hell about something Tyler only knew a little about. Caring, obviously. Took no bullshit. A straight talker—not the kind of guy who'd lie to protect Tyler's feelings.

Goddamn, he was appealing, but for all Tyler knew, he

had no interest in anything longer-term. He'd pretty clearly told Tyler that there would be no more fucking around while they were in a doctor-patient relationship.

"Something you wanna tell us?" Josh prompted, pretending to elbow Tyler just to get him to flinch.

"Asshole," Tyler groaned. "I wish."

He felt guilty for just a moment at evading the question. After all, he could tell these guys anything. They wouldn't interfere or push him.

But Alec's job… it clearly scared him shitless to have anyone else know about their indiscretion. It could put his job at risk if the wrong person overheard. Tyler couldn't break that trust, even if these were the guys he trusted most in the world.

And it was way too early to call their relationship *anything*. Not until he'd healed, and he found out if Alec wanted to try anything longer-term, and he was thinking clearly himself. Maybe this was all an outlet for his frustration at not being able to do anything useful in his life.

Rushing things wouldn't work. Slow and steady won the race. Well, maybe not *slow*… fast and steady.

Reliable. That's what he had to be—reliable. And reliable meant not breaking Alec's trust, even if Alec never found out that he'd done it. Which meant keeping *them* t himself for a bit longer.

Tyler was going to be so damn reliable it blew Alec away.

CHAPTER
Ten

ALEC

"Hey, boss. You didn't think I forgot, did you?" Rosie shot him a grin as she locked the front door of the clinic.

Alec pretended not to know what she was talking about as he hung up his white coat on a hallway hook. "Forgot what?"

"Nice try, birthday boy. I avoided embarrassing you all day, you know." Rosie pointed at the desk.

Oh, God. A card and a wrapped box sat there. The box even had a shiny silver bow on it.

Alec pretended he wasn't touched, like he did every year. "Hmph. I thought I'd finally laid low for long enough."

"That's what my recurring calendar events are for," Rosie informed him with a merciless grin. She never let his birthday go by without giving him a gift. Unlike some secretaries, she didn't even take it out of the petty cash.

"Ugh," Alec sighed, rolling his eyes dramatically as he headed over to sit on the edge of the desk. "I guess I have to say thank you, too. Take Monday morning off."

That was the other half of their usual exchange—the

chance to sleep in on Monday morning every now and then. In return, she made sure the office was organized on Friday afternoon for him to find everything until she got in at lunchtime.

He had no idea what he'd do without her, frankly.

"Oh, you didn't have to," Rosie teased, grinning.

"Yeah, I do. Can't have you running off to some other therapist." He winked, then opened the card.

It was a sweet card with an even sweeter message.

Alec—

Roll your eyes all you want, your heart is a lot bigger than you want to let on. It's a real joy to work with you day to day.

I hope you find every happiness.

Rosie

She signed the card every year with that last part, and Alec had always figured it was a general wish for his wellbeing.

Now, though, he was starting to wonder—*had* he found every happiness? Or was there more waiting for him?

There had to be. He just wasn't sure what. No, he knew what—he didn't know *how*.

If he came out and lost his business, it put Rosie's job at risk as well as his own. If he didn't, he'd just keep collecting cards from her every year, growing older and lonelier. Most years, this card and gift were the only ones he got. This year was no exception.

No, he was *not* going to be a sad loser on his birthday.

Instead, Alec smiled at Rosie. "Thanks, darling."

He found himself swept into a hug. "Of course. I mean it. You better get that heart on the market sometime soon, you know."

"Or I'll be an old maid?" Alec joked, his eyes on the present as he unwrapped it.

"No. It's never too late. But you'll miss out on years you could have had."

Rosie was only in her early forties, but to an only now thirty-year-old, her advice had proved invaluable time and time again. She was probably right now, too.

"Yeah." Once Alec opened the box, he blinked. An envelope lay inside. "Are we doing the box within a box thing?"

"We are. It increases the anticipation," Rosie informed him. "More bang for the birthday present buck."

"Oh. That's thoughtful of you." He rolled his eyes.

Rosie grinned shamelessly. "I know."

When he finally slid the envelope contents out into his hand, Alec paused, then chuckled. Tickets for the opera. "Thanks."

"There's two. You better invite that nice boy along."

Alec cleared his throat and pocketed the envelope, suddenly busy finding his jacket and car keys. "He's not really the opera type…"

"You never know. You might broaden his horizons," Rosie said. She had that evil plan look in her eye, and Alec figured it was best to escape quickly.

"Yeah. I'll think about it. See you tomorrow."

Alec was halfway to his car before he realized what Rosie's trick had been: making him admit there *was* someone.

Damn it, she totally knew.

He sighed and let himself smile. She was one of the few people who understood him, after spending so much time around him every week. And she wasn't going to ask questions until he was ready to share… but she wasn't going to let him sit around and let a good thing sail past, either.

What if he could have that kind of relationship with a guy? But with romance, and sex, and all that lifelong commitment stuff?

He couldn't deny he wanted it… but he also couldn't have it. A situation that felt familiar to him, after the last decade of going it alone.

Alec chewed his lip for the whole drive home, trying to keep his mind away from his family. Most days he barely thought about them. Christmases and birthdays were the hardest. Even if he didn't have a boyfriend, he wasn't trying to force himself into the role they wanted him to play, and that was worth it.

You don't get to have it all, Alec, he told himself. *That's just the way it is.*

It didn't stop his mind wandering to yesterday's appointments after he opened the bottle of red in the fridge. Well, not all of them… one in particular.

Tyler had been in to see him again, and it had been perfectly professional. Yeah, the chemistry between them was still there, but Tyler had been caught up in his frustration and spending all his attention learning the exercises Alec taught him. Alec had tried to appreciate that Tyler was making his job easier and respecting the boundaries between his love life and work life.

But somehow, he still wasn't satisfied. There was no way out of this. No matter what he did, it didn't seem to be the right answer.

He could go for a run, or he could finish this bottle. The group he'd been out with a few times was friendly, but at arms-length, and he didn't always feel like talking to people on the trails.

Maybe biking was where it was at. He'd always wanted to try getting into it recreationally—and he was another year older. He should get off his ass and do something about that.

After half a bottle of wine, he admitted to himself that he wanted company. He could pretend it was his ideal choice to be alone on his birthday, but if he were honest with himself, it wasn't.

Grindr didn't hold much appeal today, though. Staring at the grid of faces did nothing for him, so he closed the app and sighed. He couldn't bring himself to invite over someone for something soulless and cold.

The doorbell rang.

Couldn't be Rosie—they rarely saw each other outside work. *Fedex?* he wondered. He couldn't remember ordering anything.

The last person he expected on his doorstep was Tyler, grinning at him like he had every right to be there.

"O-Oh. Uh. Hi." Alec's mind blanked for a moment. Had he forgotten he'd invited Tyler over? Oh, God. He was in sweatpants and a t-shirt—real moping clothes—not even anything nice. Had he tidied the kitchen in a day?

"Hey," Tyler greeted casually. "So, a little birdie told me it was your birthday today."

The pieces clicked into place.

Fuck. Alec was going to have to talk to Rosie. She couldn't encourage this... this stupidity that seemed to take over his reason and logic whenever Tyler was around. It was hard enough stopping himself.

"Oh, she did, did she?" Alec shook his head with a rueful smile and stepped aside to let Tyler in.

"Hope I'm not interrupting anything." Tyler gave a wry smile and glanced up and down Alec.

Alec blushed, suddenly acutely self-conscious of the worn-out old sweatpants. "Uh. Just me and a bottle of Merlot."

"Merlot's good for necking." Tyler gave him a smirk, and just like that, the fragile wall that Alec had built in their session yesterday crashed down again.

"We can't—I can't—this isn't..." Alec stuttered, then cleared his throat. Tyler was gazing at him, waiting patiently for him to finish. He drew himself up, envisioning himself in a white coat.

A position of authority, and one he had to live up to.

"I can't engage in a sexual relationship. You know that. Even this is a little out of bounds."

"There's no such thing as a little out of bounds." Tyler's grin was a challenge as much as acknowledgement. "It's either in or out."

"I'm firmly out of bounds."

Tyler nodded. "I know. Doesn't mean I can't keep you company. The flirting's a free bonus. Nobody should be by themselves on their birthday... unless they really wanna be. And something about that Merlot tells me you don't."

Just like that, with his easygoing nature and half-smile, Tyler sliced through his guard once again. Alec hesitated, then closed the front door. "If you're sure."

The tension broke, and Tyler gave him a grand smile. "*And* I even got you something, so you can't throw me out until you open it."

"I won't throw you out," Alec snorted, but he laughed, too, and headed for the kitchen. "You shouldn't have."

Tyler sat on the couch, and Alec tried his best not to

think about what else they'd done on that couch. "It's not much, trust me," Tyler said, waving a hand. "I didn't wanna go all *thirteen roses and one of them's plastic* on you. That's probably a little out of bounds," Tyler winked.

Goddamn, he could get under Alec's skin. Alec tried not to let the heat rise in his cheeks as he headed for living room and kitchen. "Wine?"

"No necking?"

"I'm choosing to ignore that. And we're not drinking straight from the bottle, whatever the hell you drivers do on the podium," Alec warned him, shaking an empty glass at him.

He already felt lighter than he had all day. Something about Tyler just put him at ease, and he still couldn't put a finger on it.

Boy, did he want to, though.

Tyler grinned. "Fine, fine."

When they each had a full glass, Tyler handed over a little silver box.

"This better not be earrings. Or any other jewelry," Alec laughed. "That is definitely inappropriate."

Tyler glanced south meaningfully. "*Any*? Oh, that's probably inappropriate, too."

"Is thirty the right age to have a mid-life crisis and a Prince Albert? Count me out, I'm twenty-nine for the second time," Alec shivered.

When Tyler laughed, his voice seemed to fill the space with something rich and warm and comforting. However cocky his attitude, his very presence seemed to wrap around Alec, taking the stress and anxiety and loneliness away. He seemed like he was in charge and knew exactly what he was doing.

Alec distracted himself by opening the box, then blinked. It was a little racing car keyring.

"See? Totally appropriate," Tyler said playfully.

Alec wasn't sure if he was relieved or disappointed. He didn't seem to know what the hell his heart was doing lately, anyway. Not since meeting Tyler. "That's cute. Thanks."

"Now you can think of me every time you open a door." Tyler gave him a significant glance, grinning broadly.

Alec covered his face for a moment and started to laugh. He should have seen that coming, but only Tyler could make it sound so… well, *smooth*. "And what door do you want me to open?"

"Back door, front door, the door to your heart…" Tyler's grin was wicked.

"I knew you were gonna be trouble," Alec said, rolling his eyes as he set aside the box. "I shouldn't have let you talk me into…" he trailed off, gesturing around. He didn't really know where that point had been going. Tyler's smile was too distracting. *Pull it together, man.*

"The hot-as-hell sex? Friendship? Nothing wrong with those," Tyler told him. "Either, or both together. We don't have to date, if that's not your thing."

"I don't know if it's my thing." Alec found himself talking before he even thought about what he was going to say. Something about Tyler made him take his guard down, and for the first time, he didn't even mind. "Like I said—dated closeted guys way too long. It feels stupid, but I just can't do it. I don't know relationships."

"Right. That's fair. Even without your job guidelines and whatever, I wouldn't date me," Tyler laughed.

"No, I would." Alec almost clapped a hand over his mouth when the words came out so fast. "I mean, um." He grabbed his wine glass, desperate for something to do that wasn't either saying too much, or staring at Tyler like a lovelorn puppy.

"You mean?" Tyler prompted, watching him like he was genuinely interested in the answer.

Maybe that was what attracted Alec to Tyler… all these contradictions.

Tyler had, at first, acted like he was trying to get into Alec's pants. But he'd already done that and he *still* acted like that. He flirted, but he backed off when Alec told him to. But then he pushed forward a little more, like he wasn't going to give up.

It added up to a picture that was both exciting and terrifying: Tyler liked him.

"I mean, um… It's… I'm not used to… We're both not in a position, you know?"

Tyler's expression flickered, then pinched as he frowned. He glanced away for a moment. "Good point. It *is* stupid of me."

"I didn't say that." Alec found himself touching Tyler's thigh, and it was all he could do to keep his touch there instead of wandering up. "I just… need to respect myself."

Tyler's lips quivered in a little smirk. "I gave up on that ages ago. I like sex. I'm fine with that."

"No, no. I don't mean I'm ashamed of *being a slut*," Alec laughed. "I've worked my way through all those gross ideas. I like sex, too. It's more that… I keep telling myself different stories about what I want, or what I'm gonna do or not do, and then someone pretty comes along and bats his lashes… and this was the worst one yet. I've never slept with a current patient. Ever. But you…" Alec trailed off, blowing out a sigh. "I can't even regret it, but I feel like I should."

Tyler stayed attentive the whole time, listening to his words. Finally, he nodded. "No, that makes sense. If we're being honest, I shouldn't... you know, rush into anything, too. I've got a hell of a career. It doesn't make for good relationships."

"But friends, right?" Alec murmured. "I know it's inappropriate—"

"Shut up," Tyler laughed, pressing a finger against Alec's lips.

Oh, fuck. The way their knees and arms brushed as they sat side by side was irresistible enough. Adding in that touch —the firm, callused finger against Alec's soft lips? Alec wanted Tyler so badly he could taste it.

"Mm?" Alec grunted.

Tyler dropped his hand, resting it on Alec's thigh for a moment. "It's the least inappropriate option. I don't wanna just walk away yet. It's this, or do something you sound like you wanna avoid."

"No," Alec agreed, his voice soft. When had they started talking like this—so softly it seemed like neither of them wanted to shatter the atmosphere between them? It felt right, though. Intimate. "We'll do this, then."

Tyler squeezed Alec's thigh, then drew a breath like he was trying to control himself. It made Alec's skin prickle with attraction, and the desire to hear his hoarse breaths against Alec's ear...

Tyler lunged for the remote, startling Alec into a gasp. "There's a race. I'll show you, if you want. Do you know much?"

"Not much," Alec admitted, drawing a sigh of relief. Thank God Tyler wasn't staring into Alec's eyes anymore, or he might have kissed him. They'd been a few seconds away from contradicting everything Alec had told Tyler. "I'd like to learn."

The atmosphere slowly settled, but the charge in the air never seemed to fully dissipate as the next hour wore on and Tyler explained what was going on to Alec.

Racing had seemed kind of boring on TV to him before, but hearing Tyler's point of view suddenly made it real.

It wasn't just little dots going around a track now. It was fine-tuned machines, huge teams of people, constantly competing at terrifying speeds. It was nerve-racking to watch the close calls and breakdowns, and the minor accidents that did occur.

Alec suddenly realized—not that he hadn't known before, but it had never really sunk in—that Tyler's accident had probably been broadcast live to the world. His friends and family had had to watch his car being crushed.

More than anything else, it was enough to give Alec pause. He could help Tyler get back onto the track again, but listening to Tyler talk about his sport, it was clear where his heart lay.

It ran on motor oil and elbow grease, and it wasn't gonna stop for him.

Could he do that? Stand by as someone he cared about threw himself into this chaos over and over again, helpless to do anything but watch?

Alec wasn't sure, but his admiration for Tyler climbed several notches by the time they called it a night.

"Thanks for having me over," Tyler told him as they reached the door.

Alec cracked a grin. "Southern gentleman indeed," he teased, kicking his shoes out of the way and leaning on the wall. "Thanks for coming over, though."

It had been a way better night than he'd ever expected, even if his mind had been running nearly as fast as those cars the whole time.

Like it was second nature, before Tyler could open the front door, they both leaned toward each other. Before Alec thought twice about it, he was kissing Tyler. By the time he realized it, he'd been kissing Tyler way too long to be appropriate, his lips softly sliding across Tyler's as their noses brushed.

Tyler was intoxicating, and heady, and addictive. Alec's hands were on Tyler's shoulders, while Tyler touched his back and waist, their bodies nestled close. The sparks of contentment that burned in his stomach would have been unfamiliar, if he hadn't felt them before—with Tyler. Every time, in fact.

As they pulled back, Alec caught his breath and Tyler's eye. *How am I gonna explain this? For fuck's sake.*

Tyler was smiling gently at him, not saying a word. He just raised his hand in a little wave. "Take care. See you later this week, huh?"

Alec nodded wordlessly, hoping his blush wasn't as deep as it felt. "See you," he managed. "Thanks again."

"Happy birthday."

When Alec closed the door, he leaned hard against it and shut his eyes. He couldn't even blame the wine when he slid down it to sit on the floor, his heart thudding so hard it felt like his body was vibrating.

Will I ever stop chasing guys who will only end up hurting me?

Alec couldn't bring himself to care, though. Just like every time he'd slipped up with Tyler, however hard he tried to make himself regret it, he couldn't.

Maybe that's what I like about him, Alec thought. *The way he lives, he has to live life without regrets.*

And maybe—just maybe—Alec could, too.

CHAPTER
Eleven

TYLER

It was race weekend in Kentucky, and the skies in Tennessee were crisp and blue, but Tyler was miserable.

The commentary had already begun, but he barely paid attention to it. It was just speculation at this point. When they checked in on each crew, they were giving explanations for people whose car knowledge was limited to forward and reverse.

Adrenaline thrummed through him like he was about to step into the car himself. Rory had already run laps on a test day to learn the circuit, but they'd given him a few more. Why? Were there new parts since the crash?

Of course there were. They would have had to rebuild most of his car after the accident. New tires, too. That would change the grip. Maybe they were giving Rory a chance to get used to the balance.

It felt like sitting outside his friends' house, watching them having fun through the living room window. Even though it was work—hard, stressful work as all of them struggled to do more than enough in less time than they needed—it was also rewarding work.

And now all he could do was sit here and watch it on TV like a goddamn rookie.

He knew he should be happy for Rory. It was the guy's big break. The commentators had already mentioned his accident, which wasn't something he wanted to be reminded of, but at least they hadn't replayed it in slow motion again.

Tyler was going to see those few seconds of slow-motion disaster in his nightmares for years to come. The split-second where he wondered if this would be it, if he'd finally pushed his luck a little too far…

"Want a beer? Or is it too early? Race is almost starting now, huh?"

"Never too early," Tyler answered, trying to stay light-hearted as Josh poked his head in the living room. "Just a Coke right now, though. Ten minutes."

"I'll get the chips."

The race would last for hours, and he didn't plan to miss a moment of it. The first few laps and the last few were all most people paid attention for. He got a lot more out of seeing the middle—the steady grind, how it affected every team's machines, how they pitted, what line they chose… It was all valuable information. Since he wasn't wearing himself to the bone today, he could use this chance to study the rest of them.

It would take a lot of buffing to make that silver lining gleam.

67. There he was—that asshole Richie.

Josh crashed next to him on the couch with two cans of Coke and a bowl of chips. "Took your meds?"

"Yeah. I don't think I need 'em anymore, but yeah," Tyler said absently, his attention focused more on the screen.

It was stupid. Staring at Richie now wasn't gonna give him any more clues about what the hell Richie had been doing nudging him. Still, Tyler couldn't stop watching him.

Josh caught on. "That's the guy who—"

"Yeah."

"You still think it was on purpose?"

Keeping up a conversation was grinding Tyler's nerves, but he took a breath and cracked open his can of Coke. He gulped a few sips. Josh was trying to be supportive. For once, he wasn't being an asshole about it, either. He'd been acting sweet and sympathetic all day.

That was what Tyler's best friends were for. These guys— Josh more than anyone—knew when to tease him for being too stupid to quit the sport, and when to shut up and hug him.

"Think so," Tyler finally said, setting the can down again and clearing his throat.

"I guess you can't prove it, though. It's easy to fuck up when you bump draft..."

"No. Not anymore." Tyler glared at Josh. "Bump drafting is easy to notice. And you can't bump and run now. The cars won't let it happen."

"So how'd it happen?"

Tyler glared at the TV now. "Fuck me if I know. I'm not an investigator."

Josh paused, then poked at the chip bowl. "Eat more. You're getting cranky."

"Fuck you, too," Tyler muttered, but he grabbed a handful of chips. They crunched in his hand, sending tiny bits across his knees and the floor.

Josh snorted. "I won't hand you any wine glasses."

"Good. I wanna remember this."

Josh didn't say anything, just kicked back on the sofa and put his feet up on the coffee table.

After a minute, Tyler grabbed the remote and turned the volume up. It was almost green-flag time. He just had to make it through four hundred laps of watching Rory race his baby without losing his shit.

"That's Richie, isn't it? Again? In 67? Or is he 69?"

It was the second time Josh had asked. Tyler knew damn well he was trying to show an interest in his race, but there were probably other ways than pointing out the guy who might have tried to kill him.

"He's fucking 67, okay? And I don't wanna hear that asshole's name again."

Josh blinked at him, then raised an eyebrow. "All right," he said, raising his hands for a moment.

"All right." Tyler folded his arms as he leaned back into the couch, his eyes fixed on the lead car. They were about three-quarters of the way through the race now, and it had been a clean one.

In fact, everyone seemed to be driving with a little more caution than usual. Maybe watching the accident—and its aftermath—had scared some of them. Or maybe it was his imagination, and the perspective of the camera.

His team was doing well. Even Rory. He felt bad thinking it, but he was glad Rory had been trailing *his* usual position.

Everything looked tamer through a lens. Even Alec had

thought so, when he'd watched the track day coverage with Tyler.

"Want a beer?"

"Course I want a fucking beer, but my doctors will get pissy at me if I do." He knew it was logical—alcohol slowed healing progress, at best, and there were the potentially dangerous interactions with his painkillers. "So, no, I don't want a beer."

"Jesus," Josh scoffed, pushing himself to his feet. He grabbed the empty Coke cans, pinching their sides and compressing them into metal disks, one at a time. "Don't fucking bite *my* head off. Watch your mouth when you're under my damn roof." He strode for the kitchen, hands full of crushed cans.

Tyler already felt sick with frustration after hours of watching the endlessly looping machines roaring around the track, and all the lucky bastards who got to drive them. Now? It was positively simmering under his skin, a rage he couldn't quite put into words, and certainly couldn't control.

But then, he quickly reminded himself, he did it in the car. He shut off emotion and focused on the physics. The mechanics. He could be a better friend than that.

When Josh returned, Tyler cleared his throat. "Sorry," he mumbled.

"Whatever, man. Don't do it again."

"Aye aye. I'm gonna call you a shithead at least three more times before I'm back on the road." Tyler tried for a grin.

Josh avoided his gaze, his eyes fixed on the screen. "Oh, he's making a move."

That drew Tyler's attention for a few seconds before he looked back to Josh.

The only thing that mattered in his life more than racing

was his friends. Without them, he never would have had the guts to go for his dream. Hell, he wouldn't have known he could do it.

They'd been the only ones crazy enough to sit with him in his beat-up old Fords, to see his karting races, to sit in the stands for hours of him slowly grinding through the laps, trying to beat the average enough to get noticed. They watched him put his neck on the line, and were there for him when he nearly broke it. They treated him like a human being, even when interviewers and fans gave him an ego. Hell, they opened their homes to him.

He kicked Josh with his good leg. "Hey, man. I mean it."

Josh flinched and spilled his beer on his lap. "Dude!"

"Oh, dude," Tyler groaned, leaning forward to grab a handful of tissues for him. "Didn't know you were that jumpy."

"Course I am." Josh mopped up his jeans. "God, now I look like I pissed myself."

"My sense of humor *is* that awesome."

Josh cracked a smile. "Some would argue that."

The screen pulled both of their attention to it in the same moment: another wreck. Looked minor—as the camera hastily cut to the wreck, there was hardly anything to see there. The commentators were losing their minds over it, though.

Josh squinted. "That ain't Ricky's work, is it?"

"Nah. He's not even nearby. Last lap. Some idiot got a little hot-footed," Tyler shrugged it off.

And then the caution flag came out.

"Shit. Overtime line," Tyler muttered. A wreck meant a caution, which meant the next flag would end the race and it was an undignified cruise to the finish. They both watched in silence as Harrison—decent driver, but nowhere near stellar, and usually finished middle of the pack—took first place after an unremarkable performance.

"Well, that was… anticlimactic." Josh winced and glanced at him.

"God, I'd be pissed if I were there," Tyler muttered. "Rory must be losing his damn mind." He almost felt bad for him.

Not bad enough to give him a shot at Bristol, though. He was feeling better now—miles better than even last week. Given another week, he could probably manage it.

All he had to do was get Alec's approval. Or just climb in the damn car himself, whether or not Alec signed off that he was ready.

Josh clapped his shoulder. "Well, I'm gonna get out of here. Hot date tonight."

"Do I need to make myself scarce?" Tyler smirked.

Josh waved it off. "Nah. His place is as good as any."

"Okay, dude. Let me know if that changes." Unlike his evening with Alec, there was a gnawing sense of something missing.

Tyler was putting it down to jealousy. He left the TV on so he could see the interviews afterward, but he felt strangely… what was the word?

Hollow? Helpless? Wistful? Something like that. Whatever it was, he didn't like the feeling.

He missed it. He missed racing, and he missed explaining the basics to Alec and having Alec actually look interested, and he missed… well, he missed not feeling sorry for himself all the damn time.

"Fuck it. Grab me a beer after all?" he called as Josh headed for the kitchen. He was getting tired after these hours of intense focus on the TV. The exhaustion that seemed to be his default setting these days was setting in again.

Josh snorted. "After all that *woe is me* shit?"

Tyler rubbed his face and gestured at the TV. "Yeah. After all that… I need one."

"Get it yourself, asshole." Josh disappeared into the kitchen, leaving Tyler alone with his thoughts.

It was something Josh would say as a joke, but even if it wasn't… yeah, he'd earned that.

Tyler pulled the couch pillow over his face, only meaning to rest for a few minutes. But the next time he pushed it off, it was dark outside, and he was alone.

A beer sat on the coffee table.

His smile froze halfway through forming. Behind the bottle, the TV was playing an interview with none other than Richie.

Of course it had to be him. Tyler grabbed the remote and turned the TV off, but the button was too soft to really mash in a satisfying manner.

Asshole. After everything, *he'd* gotten to race again today. *He'd* been just fine. Hell, *he* was probably gonna steal Tyler's sponsor out from under him if Tyler couldn't get back in the game fast enough.

Tyler couldn't let that happen. Not again.

Jealousy was a bitter taste on his tongue and an ugly look on him, but he couldn't swallow it away. Even thinking about Rory getting a chance to test himself in a real race didn't make it stop. There was no lining silver enough to make up for the points he was gonna lose in this season. No way he could make those back now.

Tyler was gonna find a way to make Richie pay.

CHAPTER

Twelve

ALEC

KNOXVILLE WAS THE KIND OF CITY WHERE YOU COULD HIDE from someone for a while, but not for a lifetime. About once a year, Alec got an unpleasant reminder of that fact, and never when he expected it.

"Fuck." He stared at the car in the parking lot of the grocery store, wishing he hadn't noticed it. Wishing he'd remembered his parents' morning routine a little better.

The vanity license plate frame—hand-painted, bought from a roadside market in Arizona on their last family road trip—made it unmistakably their little white Ford hatchback.

Now Alec had to decide if he could stomach pretending he hadn't noticed it and going inside to shop for his weekly groceries. He hated the possibility of coming face-to-face with the people who had raised him for eighteen years before tossing him out of their lives because he didn't love quite the right people.

He realized he was chewing his thumbnail. "Fuck," he muttered and dropped his hands to his lap. The old habit was so rare now that he sometimes forgot he'd once done it. It only came out again when he was near his parents—a nervous tic born of anxiety and fear.

God, it had taken years to see how fucked up it was to have felt afraid of his own parents for so long. He wasn't going to undo any of his progress by acting like he was still afraid of them.

"Fine." He yanked his keys out of the ignition, checked his parking brake, and stormed out of his car.

If he couldn't be afraid, he was going to bring his pissed-off face to the world.

Of course, that lasted about thirty seconds. As he reached the row of carts by the entrance, he stepped out of an employee's way to let him push the returned carts into the row, then offered him a smile.

God. I can't even stay mad, can I?

He'd always been bad at acting. Being anyone other than himself was too much work. He'd done it for goddamn long enough.

Plus, he was afraid of being seen as… well… angry. He didn't even know why it scared him, but it did. Alec's pleasant attitude made him popular with patients, but surely there was a limit. When guys used him for sex, he ought to be angry. When people cut him off in traffic, it wouldn't kill him to flip them the middle finger now and then.

But nope—his mask slipped off fast, and he was always just… him. Whether or not that was enough for someone else.

The first few aisles were clear, and he gradually relaxed as he gathered vegetables.

It wasn't until he crouched by the bottom shelf to pick up his favorite pasta sauce that his senses prickled. The hair stood up on the back of his neck, and he knew without looking around who must have been nearby. A moment later, he realized he was smelling his mom's perfume.

The faintly flowery scent was distinctive. Mom had always worn it to church. They picked up snacks for the Sunday school kids before church, and bought non-perishable foods for the food bank and household at the same time.

Sure enough, his mom was halfway to grabbing a bag of pasta when she caught sight of him. As they made eye contact, he kept his expression as blank as he could, even though hope rose in his chest as always.

Her expression closed off and she grabbed two bags of pasta, then turned and strode down the aisle, her head high.

And Alec's stupid fucking heart broke again, just a little. It wasn't that he hadn't expected it. It was just…

It was a stupid thing, hope. Soul-crushing and irrational and utterly unstoppable.

He blinked rapidly a few times, grabbed the pasta sauce, and straightened up, staring through the shelves of pasta. When had he last seen her face-to-face? He'd spotted his dad in the hardware store last summer. Dad had maintained the even stiffer facade of the two of them—he always pretended not to see Alec.

Just as always after one of these encounters—once or twice a year, at most—he suddenly wanted to learn poker. A poker face would give him the edge he was missing. Right now, they had hold of the knife and they were twisting it around and around in his chest with every goddamn accidental encounter.

He hated that he'd let his mom see him hopeful, and then hurt, if only for a few seconds.

"Fuck me," he muttered under his breath, realizing he'd been standing still for a good minute. As he reached the end of the aisle, he caught sight of his parents, arm in arm. They'd gotten through the checkout, and they were carrying bags out to the car.

They stopped briefly to drop a bag of pasta in the food collection box, then kept walking.

It had always bothered him: how the hell could his parents donate to the food bank when they'd made their own kid homeless and nearly hungry? If it hadn't been for his scholarship and the cheap apartment he'd found in freshman year, he would have been screwed. He'd juggled two campus jobs to pay for that plus food, and even then, he'd gone with less food than he should have at times.

They'd had plenty of support from his grandparents— only two of whom were still alive, but both of whom had taken their side. Or God's side, as they would have put it.

When the hell had any of *them* ever known that pain?

Alec turned on his heel and headed back to grab two more bags of pasta.

He'd almost forgotten what this particular black hole of loneliness felt like.

Way back when, this might have left Alec in a depressed funk for days or weeks. He'd wasted a lot of time feeling like crap about himself, and he was done wasting more time now. Only school and then his career had pulled him along at first. Getting to do something helpful, physical, and fascinating had been his lifeline.

Most importantly, it was something to help people and quiet the voice that still echoed around his mind sometimes

—selfish bastard, you only think of yourself. As if he'd been gay just to inconvenience them.

He drummed his fingers on the steering wheel as he stared at the front of his parents' church.

Sunday service would be under way now. He'd deliberately done a few circuits around Knoxville before driving to the church parking lot, lest he cause a commotion. But a small part—okay, a pretty big part of him—wanted to do exactly that.

Did he want to walk in and ask the new reverend—some Rev. Paul Goodson, apparently—for forgiveness? Hell, no. He refused to apologize for love.

Maybe this new reverend would be reasonable about it and understand *his* point of view. Or maybe he'd be worse. God only knew. *Hah. God,* he thought. He kept his hands on the steering wheel so he didn't go for the door handle, and… lose the battle of will going on within him right now.

When Alec probed his thoughts deeper, they didn't feel charitable. A vindictive, bitter need for something was eating away at him. He wanted to make a scene and be inconvenient for his parents. Alive and happy. Successful and good and smart. All the things they'd said he wouldn't be.

But what would that solve? For whatever stupid reason, his parents had no love left for him. It was like dipping a bucket into an empty well, hearing it rattle and clatter around as he desperately searched for a drop.

No. Alec had to find his own wellspring of acceptance and approval—somewhere deep inside himself. He could usually tap into it and quiet the memories of angry, heartfelt, *heartbreaking* words. Only sometimes did this uglier, needy side of him come out.

He closed his eyes and shook his head, letting go of the wheel and slumping in his seat.

It wasn't even love from his parents that he was looking for, or he could show up at their front step. But a church was supposed to be—*was*, to some lucky bastards—a community. Somewhere to feel accepted, and safe, and home.

He wanted to find that feeling of being at home and hold on with both hands.

Sure, he had a house of his own now, but that was nowhere near the same thing, and he knew it. Over the past few years, Alec could remember fairly often staying up late at night, alone and lost in his own thoughts.

For just a moment, he remembered hanging out with Tyler. Comfortably sprawled on the couch together, listening to him explaining what was happening as cars went round and round the track. Drinking wine together, laughing about stupid commercials.

Something like that. But… with the right guy. Someone who'd stay around forever.

Fuck. He didn't want just any old guy, though. His fantasy wasn't about just "some guy" taking notice of him anymore. It was Tyler that he wanted to stay around forever. And given his career, that was unlikely.

Okay, that explained this. It wasn't about his parents at all. He was freaking out because he liked the guy.

Alec started the car and pulled out for another round of aimless driving, this time setting a course for the edge of Knoxville, where it was a bit more peaceful. If he kept driving for long enough, he'd end up in Gatlinburg and then the Smokies.

He remembered his mom telling him, years and years ago, that he'd been a fussy baby to get to sleep. They'd often put him in the car and driven him around the neighborhood. It had been the only foolproof way to calm him down, she said.

How the worm turned. Now he was driving himself around to calm down after seeing the people who ought to have loved him—or at least tried.

Alec's hands tightened on the wheel. He wasn't that unlovable, was he?

He turned up the music, drumming his fingers along to the classic rock station as the speed limit picked up and fields flew by. He was surrounded by farmland before long. Which farm was Tyler staying on? And with whom? His parents? He'd mentioned something about it, but that was it.

At least it was a beautiful day for a drive, now that he'd passed most of the Sunday drivers in their fancy classic cars. The Smokies loomed behind flower-studded spring meadows, sometimes disappearing behind copses of trees putting out fresh spring buds.

The anxiety tightening his chest gradually lessened, and he even took a risk and rolled down the window, hoping he didn't get a noseful. But, soothing though it was, the vast scenery also amplified the emptiness that thudded strangely in his chest.

Alec was still lonely, and he still wanted Tyler, consequences or not.

This wasn't going away, which meant one thing in his experience: grabbing it with both hands and figuring out what the hell it was.

That's it. Time to decide.

As soon as Tyler was out of his care, Alec would ask him out. But no sooner had he thought that than he realized that his opportunity—those opera tickets—was coming up a lot sooner.

The opera was just next week. And could he really wait two or three or six more weeks for Tyler to decide he'd had enough physical therapy? He hadn't been able to resist Tyler yet, after all.

"Okay, Alec," he murmured out loud, slowing down when he reached a pull-off that overlooked the mountains. They were startlingly close now—had he really driven this far while sorting through the mess of thoughts and feelings? "Time to make the call."

He'd make a terrible referee, always able to see the other side of every decision but never quite sure which was the right one.

When it came to his life, he had even less of an idea. All he could do was follow his heart, which was telling him one thing—loud and clear.

"That's it. I'm gonna ask him out."

CHAPTER
Thirteen

TYLER

TYLER'S FIRST WARNING—HIS *ONLY* WARNING—WAS THE forwarded email that hit his inbox at six in the morning. The subject line read simply, CALL ME.

Tyler had woken up at four to take painkillers and dropped back to sleep, so everything was hazy as he struggled to see who the email was from.

Oh. Shit. It was Sarah, the PR person for his racing team.

He clicked the email and scrolled down, and everything felt unreal for a few long seconds. There was something to do with an alert for a match of a new search result online with his name and the word *gay*.

Tyler hated that his first reaction when he saw the word was a gnawing worry in the pit of his stomach. That had never been the case growing up, or even getting started racing. Not until his career took off.

And it wasn't like it was a secret. An open secret, of sorts. Nobody had ever directly asked him who he dated. Everyone had just assumed, and he'd been fine to let them keep assuming, if they were too backward-thinking to ask.

The only people he proactively told were his teammates, the owner, and PR people. Not even to ask if it was okay, just in a *hey, just so you know* way. Still, it felt like the way someone would disclose something stupid—criminal charges, or getting drunk and starting a bar fight.

"Fuck," he muttered under his breath as he clicked the link and a racing blog came up. Not a tiny, one-man operation, either. This was one of the bigger bloggers out there—a guy who had a team of four or five bloggers working for him.

Tyler instantly knew that this was who Bobby had been trying to warn him about. LeeN, as he was known online, had already earned himself a reputation. He'd slipped past security a few times at events just to get insider photos, and he often posted pieces about drivers' relationships and life stories that were clearly clickbait to get attention.

TY-JO CRASH INVESTIGATORS: "TOO GAY TO DRIVE!"

Knowing LeeN, he'd change the headlines a few times to try to get the most attention. Frankly, the subheading— TYLER JOSEPH SUCKS AT MORE THAN DRIVING— would have made a better headline. Or the heading below that, which read, (MARCSON'S DICK?) Jesus, how many headings did this article need?

And like the team owner was remotely his type. Tyler rolled his eyes and carefully pushed himself to sit upright in the pile of pillows, his palms sweating as he dialed Sarah's number.

"Hey, Ty. You're up early."

"Sarah. Yeah. My ribs. Ain't getting much sleep," Tyler managed, his sentences almost choked. Whoa. He was more anxious than he'd expected.

"Take it easy," she said, sounding way too wide awake.

"Shit. Is it a… big thing?"

"Well, that's the part that really gets me. Did you read it?"

"LeeN's stuff?" Tyler snorted. "I don't like fiction."

She chuckled. "There's just a bunch of vague stuff about you staying with a guy friend of yours, and being seen with guys all the time, and someone who came forward saying they hooked up with you at a party once. The usual speculation and gossip."

"Oh, good—"

"*But,*" she continued firmly, making his heart sink before he even had a chance to feel relieved, "there's more this time."

"Shit. What is it?"

"It got posted to a fan forum. There's a seven-page thread talking about it already."

"That sounds like a lot. How big is a thread?" Tyler asked. "Is that a lot of people? Like a score?"

Sarah stifled a snort. "Ty, a thread is… never mind. It's an internet thing. Yeah, lots of people. Several people confirming stories, including one from high school who says he knows for sure you're gay. But a lot of the posters are women, your core demographic."

More than anything else, that gave Tyler a moment's pause. A driver wasn't just hired because he was good in the car. Sure, he had to be able to drive, but these days he also had to be charismatic, or at least reasonably attractive, or have some kind of charm. Something that made people want to watch him.

If he lost that…

"Oh."

"They like you more now. You're extra-cool. They have something in common with you, you know?"

"I do?" Tyler's mind spun. This was all a little too much, a little too fast.

"They like your dick, you like other guys' dicks." Sarah was as blunt as ever.

Tyler laughed sharply and gasped for breath, pressing his hand to his rib. Stupid thing. "Liking dick... means... they like me more?"

Sarah was clearly trying to decide how to explain this internet thread to him. "Yeah, sure. That's the summary."

"I thought... it would be a bigger deal than that," Tyler mumbled. "I'm the first... I mean... you know!"

"I know," Sarah agreed. "And we can't rely on the mood staying this positive, but if you get ahead of the curve..."

"And out myself?" They'd had this conversation before. Tyler didn't care who knew, but he wanted someone to fucking *ask* him. To act like it was an equally valid, normal possibility. Not just assume he was straight and clutch their pearls if he wasn't. And *definitely* not to put the burden on him to admit it in public like a dirty secret.

Sarah didn't see eye-to-eye with him, but she was also interested in avoiding having their team be the talk of the racing world for personal reasons, so they'd agreed. Until now, anyway.

"If you don't want it to be a secret, you gotta talk about it, man. That's how secrets work."

"Fuck that bullshit." Tyler was just as open with the women around him as he was with the guys, despite the gentlemanly reputation. They got each other. She didn't spare his feelings, and he wasn't going to treat her like a delicate flower, either.

"I know it sucks." Sarah sighed. "But someone's gonna ask for a comment. This thread isn't just dying off like usual. It's getting too big. All it takes is one ballsy blogger to ask and then that guy—even if it's LeeN himself—gets the scoop."

Tyler squirmed to get the pillow more comfortable behind his head. He hated that she was so right. He'd always planned to say it to the first person who asked like it wasn't a big deal, but they might treat it otherwise.

"I hate people," he muttered under his breath.

She chuckled shortly. "I know, hon. I woke up from a damn good dream for this."

"Sorry," Tyler winced.

He didn't want to make it sound all about him when it *did* affect the rest of the team. The guys had all been great to him —respectful of his boundaries, way more so than the media. They never asked awkward questions about where he got to at afterparties, and they didn't use him as their token gay friend.

If reporters couldn't get through to him, they might start hounding the others, which would put them in an awkward position. *No comment*ing the whole thing made it sound like there was something to hide. Lying made them look bad, even if it was to protect him. And telling the truth wasn't theirs to do.

"So," Sarah spoke up, and he cut her off.

"I'll do it. Whatever. I'll do it my style, though. No interview, no press conference, none of that bullshit."

"What are you planning?" Sarah asked cautiously.

"I don't know yet." Tyler grinned, his heart suddenly light. "But I'll think of something."

"Oh, lord. This must be what your spotter feels like."

Tyler laughed. "Probably. I'll call you later."

"No chance of a call *before* you do anything?"

"None. I'll let you know afterward, though, so you aren't

on the edge of your seat and keeping a Big Brotherly eye on me."

Sarah laughed. "That's all I can ask for, I guess. Bye."

Tyler tossed the phone on the bed and raised his hand to rub his face, then sighed deeply. That reminded him to take his deep breaths.

Whatever he was gonna do, it had to be at a gentle stroll.

It reminded him of something Alec had said: *No running before you can walk, and no driving before you can sit up straight.*

What would Alec do? For that matter, what about his brothers? If anyone had advice, it would be them. Yeah. That was a good starting point.

Tyler picked up his phone again, unlocked it, and opened their group chat. He had a hell of a message to write.

***

"Sorry, man. We're the extent of the damage control squad until this evening." Deen shrugged. Even the simplest motion, from him, was expressive. Maybe it was the studded leather jacket, the limp grip on his Coke glass, and the way he held himself—unapologetic and confident—that did the talking.

They were just around the corner from their usual bar. This diner was a good brunch spot when Tyler and his friends could make it out here.

Next to Deen, and across from Tyler in the booth, Oscar had his own Coke in a firm grip, his brows furrowed in a problem-solving expression. Without the other guys, there was way too much elbow room on his side of the table. It felt weird as hell.

Josh was busy leading a trail ride, since his right-hand

man was on vacation. Falcon and Leo had gone to some kind of art event in Nashville and stayed there last night to network with artsy people; Tyler hadn't really paid attention to the details. Most of the rest of them—Nico, Roman, Blane, Dustin—had day jobs.

"No, man. Having you guys to talk is…" Tyler trailed off. A lifesaver? Might sound overdramatic, even if these two spoke primarily in overstatements and gestures. "Great," he settled on, even though the word fell flat.

"It's good for me to get out of the house," Oscar admitted. "No classes today—we're between semesters. If if weren't for this, I'd just lounge around in leggings all day until Roman came home."

Deen laughed. "I know that feeling. Sometimes I feel bad about Nico going to work every day when I just sit around writing songs in my underwear and eating Cheerios."

Tyler snorted with laughter. "Must be nice to hang out at home sometimes, though." They'd both had careers that took them on the road too much when they'd started dating their significant others.

Deen still toured, but less frequently now, and he hadn't committed to any world tours. Oscar, formerly a pro dancer, ran his own dance studio now, which kept him closer to home.

But that wasn't an option for Tyler. Quitting his job sure as hell wasn't happening, and there was no way to do what he did and stay closer to home. The biggest race tracks were dotted across the country, and the schedule was grueling— races every week, usually.

Racing season was ten months long, with only December and January off; otherwise, he had just a couple days off every month to come back home and relax. He'd more than once considered just giving up his apartment and crashing with different friends when he wasn't racing, his time off was so scarce.

But that included afterparties and events that, strictly speaking, he didn't *have* to do. He could scale it back a little. Of course, his visibility would suffer, which affected his sponsorships...

"Yo, man. Ty. You're gone," Deen laughed.

"Shit. Sorry," Tyler laughed under his breath. "I was just thinking."

"About?"

Tyler really didn't want to answer that honestly. "So I made friends with my physical therapist. I was talking about my work situation with him. I might ask if he's free."

"If he knows more about the sport than us, that'd be great," Oscar said and nodded. He pushed away the plate with a few last uneaten fries and gestured to the waitress for refills all around. "You're always making new friends. Surely some of them will have your back, huh?"

Tyler didn't take that to heart. He was always mentioning different guys, it was true, but most of them weren't exactly *friends*. Acquaintances and rivals from the racing world, the whole team of engineers and mechanics and admin that surrounded him, partygoers... not friends.

"Oh, I think so. Some," Tyler said, shrugging. "But nobody wants to stick their neck out at the wrong time. And you know the viewer demographics. I don't know if the time is right for me to be... well, me."

"If it's not, do you really wanna stick around?" Deen was blunt and intent on Tyler's reaction, barely glancing at the waitress as he thanked her for the refills. When they were alone again, he leaned forward. "Because then you're gonna be *that queer*, you know? Or you're gonna be less *you* to be more palatable. And people spot that easy. That's one reason why I've been so vocal about being bi. I want my fans to see a bit of me, even if there's a whole machine of advertising and branding at work around me. Selectively me."

Tyler flinched and looked down at the table. It had been enough of an open secret that he already felt like it sometimes. "Yeah. Good point. I've been selectively me—but it's starting to get noticeable, like a..." He gestured, pressing his thumbs and the tips of his other fingers together. "A hole in the middle of my life."

"Conspicuous by its absence," Oscar murmured.

It took Tyler a second to wrap his brain around the words, but then he nodded. "Exactly. I mean, not having anyone to date is fine. Besides, how would that even work for me?"

They exchanged looks. "Depends on you, babe," Oscar hummed, stretching out and lacing his hands behind his head. "Roman and I talked about being open because he was on the road all the time."

"You did?" Deen looked surprised as he glanced over.

"Yeah, sure. We decided not to, and then he ended up switching to short-haul flights so he isn't away so much. But it's an option."

Tyler sighed. "It's not even that." He shook his head. "I mean, how the hell do I trust my own instincts about guys? All I do is fuck them and move on. And then how do I decide who's worth... going through all this media circus for? And you guys have been on the road."

Deen nodded, fingers laced as he tapped his folded hands on the table slowly.

"It's not just wanting more sex. You know how

goddamn… lonely it gets." Tyler paused for a second, brows furrowing. He hadn't expected these words to spill out—especially not before a few beers. He shut himself up before he could say more, swallowing a few mouthfuls of Coke.

Oscar straightened up. "Yeah. I know. But I'll tell you something—the loneliness was always manageable. It sucked, and there were some long fucking nights—or fuck-less nights, if you prefer." He smirked.

Deen snorted. "Not many of those for me!"

"Yeah, yeah," Tyler laughed at him. Most of them had had their fair share of no-strings-attached sex. Yet fewer of them were keeping it up. God, all of them had finally found someone they were staying with for more than a few weeks… and all of them seemed *happy* about it.

It seemed far less weird to wrap his head around now that he'd met Alec.

Oh, hell, no.

"But," Oscar continued, talking over them. "It got a hundred times worse after I started to fall for Roman."

"Gross. Most of us are happy to send his loud mouth to another continent for a while." Tyler grinned cheerily as Oscar leaned over the table to shove him.

"You *know* what I mean," Oscar scoffed.

"Yeah. I do." *I've been missing him even though we haven't hung out much. Like when I was with him, it was... something different, yet familiar. Like home.*

"Fuck," Tyler muttered under his breath and stared down at his Coke, stirring the straw around and poking at the ice cubes in the glass with the end.

"What?" Deen prompted when he didn't clarify.

Tyler tried to pull his thoughts together. He couldn't out Alec when Alec wasn't even out—especially with the job concerns. It felt strange keeping him a secret, but at the same time, they hadn't even come to any agreement about what would happen after he was out of Alec's care as a patient.

He wasn't gonna spill his heart over a guy who might not even want something serious.

"Well," he said slowly, trying to keep it to vague, general suggestions. "I mean, if I'm out now… anyone I meet is in the spotlight."

"But then they won't have to hide, which feels worse," Oscar murmured.

Tyler paused and then nodded. He couldn't argue that logic.

"And," Deen picked up the thread, leaning forward. "Man, when you meet the one, you might resist it—with everything you've got. But don't throw away a good thing 'cause it scares you. You would never get behind a wheel if you listened to that voice. Your relationship could be just as good as your job."

Oscar murmured, "We have a saying in the dance world. I tell my students that if you put half your ass in, you'll get your whole ass hurt. Trying to protect yourself means you'll jump wrong—so you'll land wrong."

He should know. Oscar had been sidelined from a hell of a high-flying career by a stupid little accident, just stepping slightly wrong on a staircase. Tyler felt bad for the guy. At least in his sport, cars could be adapted to just about any injury.

Assuming you hadn't collected a bunch at once in a spectacular high-speed crash, of course.

"So, you're saying… put my whole ass into it," Tyler said, smirking.

Deen laughed. "Yeah, man. Just the tip never satisfied anyone."

"We're gonna get kicked out if you keep talking that loud," Oscar scolded, but he was grinning.

Tyler got what Oscar was trying to say, though. If he half-assed this, he was just gonna hurt them both. Same on the track, really. Every action had to be decisive. There was no room to wander between lines or understeer at the wrong moment.

The right move always felt a little like oversteer if you were listening to that voice of caution, but he hadn't before.

Why start now?

Fourteen

ALEC

It was a casual invitation, but Alec understood exactly what it was supposed to mean.

"Do you want to meet some of my friends this evening? I mean, if you don't have plans already."

Alec gripped the phone so tightly it hurt as he paced between his kitchen and living room. He tried to match Tyler's tone—casual, but not dismissive. "Tonight? Yeah, I'm free. That's no problem."

"We've got kind of a… work problem of mine to talk about."

"Oh?"

Tyler sighed. "Some gossip blog outed me. No proof, but the usual—saying it like they know for sure. Apparently this one's catching on, in… threads on the internet."

Alec choked back a laugh. "In threads?"

"There's a thread of many people talking. That's what Sarah told me."

"Do you even internet, bro?" Alec would have laughed if the situation weren't so serious.

"Barely," Tyler grumbled. "This is why. It's all a toxic wasteland of… gossip and rumors and lies."

"Yeah, man," Alec sympathized. "That's shitty. You want me there? Given… you know…"

"If you don't mind. I mean, it's sort of… relevant to you. To us. Or whatever." Tyler was speaking cautiously, which was a rarity for him. He seemed to prefer the bull-in-a-china-shop charge.

"Or whatever," Alec echoed, chuckling. "It is relevant, yeah. Are we going to talk about that *us* beforehand, or…?"

Tyler hastily said, "I haven't told them."

"Oh. Right." Alec was pretty sure he was relieved. Right?

"So, um, at our own pace… once I'm healed up and whatever… we can think about stuff." There was a pause, and then Tyler huffed a quick breathy laugh. "I'm no good at this shit on the phone, man. Let's talk face-to-face."

The realness just spilled out every which way. Tyler was very "what you see is what you get," and Alec appreciated the hell out of that.

"Yeah, of course. Tonight, what time?"

"I've been hanging out with my buddies all day. I figure around seven, most of them should be around. Not everyone at once—God, you'd run away screaming if we did."

Alec's palms were sweating. He wiped them on his jeans and grimaced. *No reason to feel anxious,* he told himself. "Why? Are they that scary?"

"Nah. Just a lot of them. But only four or five can make it tonight. Short notice and whatever. I'll text you the address," Tyler added. "And… thanks. I mean, I doubt there's guys hiding in bushes with cameras. I'm not *that* famous. But if you'd rather not be seen…"

"Fuck that," Alec said, and he surprised even himself with

how strong his voice was. He cleared his throat, glancing in the shiny oven range hood. He couldn't see himself well enough to confirm it, but he could feel the blush burning his cheeks. "I mean," he hastily continued, "I'm not gonna ditch your ass if you've been outed. That's just... that's shitty."

"It's survival." Tyler's voice was quiet, almost resigned.

"It doesn't have to be." Alec shook his head, his pacing speeding up. He spun on his heel when he reached the end of his kitchen to turn around and make for the living room again. "I mean, not for me. Not right now. Maybe a few years ago I wouldn't have been ready. But now..."

"Ready for what?" It wasn't just an innocent question. Tyler didn't even sound wary of the response he might receive. In fact, that was... hope? Something tinged his voice. Whatever he said about being bad at phone conversations, somehow they'd opened this Pandora's box, and now they couldn't close it again.

Alec seized the moment. "To take a chance. When the time is right, and the guy is right."

Tyler snorted with laughter. "I'm hardly ever right, but I act like I am."

"It's attractive, don't worry." Alec's voice almost cracked. Was this the right moment to ask him out? Or should he wait to do it face-to-face?

"Thanks, handsome," Tyler drawled. "Oops. I gotta get inside—supper's here."

Right. He was with his friends. Alec had forgotten, he was so caught up in talking to him. "Sorry. Of course, I'll let you go now."

"We'll talk later." Coming from Tyler, that was a promise, not a brush-off.

Alec's skin prickled already with anticipation. "Can't

wait." Even if the idea of meeting Tyler's friends—the people most important to him, who probably had the most influence on what he did and who he dated—was scary as fuck.

It was an opportunity.

Tyler answered, "Me neither. See you tonight."

"Bye."

"Bye," Alec chuckled awkwardly, but the line didn't disconnect yet. It was like they were playing telephone chicken, neither of them wanting to be first to hang up.

He finally jabbed the button quickly, trying to ignore the fact that he was blushing again.

Yeah. At this rate, he wasn't gonna make it a few more weeks to ask Tyler out. He'd be lucky if he made it past tonight.

He was so screwed.

———

"Everyone, this is Alec."

Alec's heart was racing sixty to the dozen as he waved at the booth of guys. Four of them already sat there, all of them reaching out to shake hands or rising to half-hug him.

One by one, he learned their names and tried his best to remember them: Leo, who was built like a brick outhouse but somehow put Alec at ease immediately with a grin; Oscar, a slender, graceful little guy with striking features; Blane, the guy with what looked like animal scratches across his cheek; Nico, who had been arm-wrestling Blane just a minute ago; and, last but not least, Deen.

Deen as in Deen Jayse, the rock star who had just gotten engaged to a guy on stage not long ago. A month or a few ago? Alec had seen it going around on Facebook.

Alec's jaw dropped, but he tried to play it cool as he shook hands like he hadn't noticed who Deen was.

Tyler snickered, not fooled for a moment. "Yeah, *that* Deen."

"Sure. Stealing the spotlight as usual," Nico hassled him, tugging Deen back down and wrapping an arm around him.

Alec laughed at the move—was he jealous? Deen was hot and all, but much less his type than… well, than Tyler. He looked around at everyone else and waved. "Hey, guys. Good to meet you all at last."

Oscar groaned theatrically. "Oh, no. It's all lies."

"Most of it is lies. Except the bits where we're all sexy bastards," Nico added, grinning and tousling his own hair.

"Oh, good point. Yes. That part is true," Oscar agreed.

"And you say I have an ego?" Tyler winked at Alec. "See where I get it?"

"Yeah. It's clearly inherited," Alec snickered and sat next to Tyler in the booth, his skin tingling pleasantly at the proximity.

"Who's the daddy?" Blane smirked. "There are like ten of us. Surely someone's the daddy around here."

Oscar shook his head. "Bad news, Blane. It's you."

Blane yelped. "What?"

"The animal daddy."

"Is that why…" Alec trailed off, touching his own cheek where Blane's scratches were.

Blane mirrored the movement, then laughed. "Oh. Yeah, I had a mild disagreement with a meerkat this morning."

"Aw, no." Alec frowned. "Aren't they sweet?"

"They're still wild animals," Blane said. "I moved too fast and he got scared. My bad."

Alec liked the attitude. He nodded. "So I take it you're a

vet or something?"

"Yep. We're all… in a hell of a weird bunch of jobs."

"This ain't the accountants' professional networking circle," Oscar laughed. "I teach dance, Nico's a park ranger, Deen's… well… Deen. Leo's a photographer. And then there's Ty."

"Alec's a physical therapist. Hell of a good one," Tyler added.

Despite his attempt to stay cool, a blush crept up Alec's cheeks at the compliment. "Thanks."

Tyler shrugged. "Wouldn't say it if it weren't true."

"Ain't that the truth," Nico chuckled. "Ty's never been one to beat around the bush. So… speaking of your job, Tyler?"

With that, the mood at the table changed subtly. Everyone straightened up and paid attention to Tyler.

"Not much to tell," Tyler said, shaking his head. "There was a blog post speculating wildly about whose dick I suck—the team owner, in case you'er wondering." He rolled his eyes and glanced over at Alec, pushing a beer his direction. "Here."

Alec laughed. "It's dangerous to go into this conversation alone. You'll need this." He took the beer.

The only guy there who'd played enough roleplaying video games to understand the joke, apparently, was Nico. He chortled heartily, a sound that made the rest of them crack up.

"I'll need a lot more than one," Tyler added. "So this internet thread got started. Apparently a bunch of people already knew—which I knew anyway, I wasn't hiding it. And then more people, mostly women, are saying they don't care."

"Aw," Alec murmured, his heart lifting. That was unexpected good news.

Deen beamed. "Yeah. A lot of people were supportive to me, too."

"Our demographics barely talk to each other on Facebook," Tyler pointed out bluntly, sipping his beer.

Deen thought about it for a moment and nodded. "Ah. Yeah."

"So Sarah—the PR person for the team—wants me to come out. I always said I wouldn't lie if someone asked, and someone's gonna ask now," Tyler finished. He looked around at the others. "So, I gotta make it official somehow."

"You want to beat the rumor mill to the presses," Alec concluded.

"Basically."

"How?"

Tyler's brows furrowed. "That's the bit I don't know."

Alec opened his mouth, then closed it quickly and glanced around at the others. *Do* not *nominate yourself as his boyfriend, Alec Lands.* He hoped the near-slip didn't show in his expression.

"How about you, like, roll yourself up in a rainbow flag like a burrito and post a super-cute Insta photo?" Deen propped his chin on his fist.

"I was gonna suggest an interview with a decent men's mag," Nico laughed, rubbing the back of Deen's neck. "Different strokes."

"Stroking himself? What?" Leo deadpanned.

Alec snickered along with the rest of them. Tyler seemed way less stressed than he'd anticipated, given their discussions about it in the past.

Tyler cast Alec a glance. "I'm just worried about people around me."

"Eh. We can take the heat," Nico brushed it off. "You figure out what you wanna do and we'll have your back."

Oscar elbowed Nico. "Most of us are out," he said slowly, as if trying to give him a chance to catch on. From the look he cast Alec, he'd figured out Tyler's concern already.

Alec blushed and waved a hand. "It's not a big deal."

"Yeah, it is."

"It really isn't." Alec shook his head. "If people are worried about catching gayness, they... well, I can live without their support."

"They don't mind straight women as physical therapists, do they?" Leo snorted. "They can deal with a dude who likes dudes, too."

"Next on the agenda: world peace," Oscar laughed. "Seriously, guys. It's a little unrealistic to think there won't be any backlash."

"Yeah." Leo was somber now. "I mean, the job thing is a big one. I was lucky that I got to go freelance. I don't know your situation," he nodded to Alec.

"Whoa. It's not about me," Alec laughed. "It's Tyler under the spotlight here." His cheeks were burning. "I'm just a... a friend."

To their credit, the rest of the table kept the knowing glances to a minimum.

Tyler cleared his throat. "And I can't just become a freelance driver. Yeah." He glanced at Leo, then back to the rest of them. "But I don't care if I get my sponsorship yanked. I'm not in it for fans, or fame. I just want to drive. My team knows that. I'll come up with something—not, like, a TV interview." He shook his head. "Maybe something on social media. And then that's it. I don't want to tell them about my personal life anyway. I haven't before now."

"That's probably smart," Alec agreed. It seemed like the least confrontational way to address Tyler's sexuality when so many people would take even this much as some kind of overly-aggressive propaganda, or comparing about him "shoving it down our throats."

Still, it rankled that other guys got to talk about their girlfriends on TV or even have them get involved in the races, but *that* wasn't crossing some kind of invisible comfort boundary for them.

Alec drowned his frustration in a few gulps of beer, letting the bitter burn soothe the heat in his chest. His throat was tight, though, so he choked and coughed.

"Hey. No dying on me here," Tyler said cheerily and clapped his back. The pat was relatively gentle.

Alec managed to catch his breath and rolled his eyes. "That's some shitty first aid, man."

"What, *please don't die* works?" Tyler laughed. "I don't know. Works for me."

Oscar sighed at them all. "Let's talk about something more cheerful. Like the wedding." He looked at Nico and Deen. "Got a date yet?"

"We're thinking late summer," Deen told them. He was suddenly smiling broadly. "I mean, at first I was thinking we'd just do a long engagement, but..."

"But his little romantic heart wants to do it ASAP," Nico added, earning a smack on the chest from Deen.

"Jerk."

"It's true." Nico smirked mercilessly. "Who knew there was such a Disney fan hiding in a little bad boy package?"

"Little?" Deen looked wounded.

"Whoa. Getting to some TMI territory there," Blane warned.

Alec was perfectly happy to sit back and listen to the guys bantering. Somehow, he felt instantly welcomed. Maybe because they'd been so quick to accept him, like he was Tyler's boyfriend or something.

No judgment, no measuring up to their expectations of him or anything. Just instant trust and inclusion in the conversation. Solidarity, without him having to out himself or talk about his childhood or any of that crap.

It was… a community.

This was what I was missing. The thought stung. In his years living here, slowly building a life for himself, he'd neglected to add friends to it.

Every time he tried joining hobby groups or talking to those around him who seemed to be attending events alone, he'd only drifted apart, or they hadn't clicked in the first place. Hell, he hadn't even gone back to the running group in the last couple weeks.

But these guys? Maybe he could hold onto them, even if Tyler wasn't his to hold.

The night passed way quicker than he expected it to once they got to drinking, talking, and laughing. "Oh, man," Alec finally groaned. "I'd better get home and leave you guys to the hardcore partying."

Tyler laughed. "I'll head home, too. It'll get hard to find an Uber who'll take me that far as it gets later. Plus, someone I know keeps saying I need to rest."

"True." Alec wagged a finger. "This isn't very restful." Fun it might be, but rest it was not.

Once they'd said their goodbyes, Alec walked Tyler to the exit, keeping an eye on him. He was still moving slowly, even if he was noticeably better than he had been in that first appointment.

He wondered if those bruises had healed. Then, he blushed at the thought. *Don't picture him without his clothes on until you're in the shower later.*

"Thanks for coming tonight," Tyler murmured. "I wanted you to meet these guys. Not just about… you know. But also because… you know."

Alec laughed. "Well, that was crystal clear."

"Shut up," Tyler groaned. "I mean, because they're important to me. And stuff. And so are you. So. You know…" he gestured, bringing both hands together.

"Are you saying you want me to bang them now?"

"No!" Tyler yelped instantly, then looked sheepish. "I mean, no. Duh."

"I know what you mean," Alec laughed. "I just wanted to see the look on your face."

"Of jealousy?" Tyler looked straight at him, tipping his chin up. He was a couple inches shorter—a compact package of sexy muscles and confidence. God, if only he weren't so damn attractive, it would be a lot easier to resist making bad decisions. "You don't have to be."

But the bad decisions just kept making themselves whenever Tyler was in eyeshot.

Alec stepped forward and Tyler met him in a kiss. For a few long seconds, the world around them slipped away. All that existed in this moment was the two of them—none of their fears, none of the uncertainties about the future, none of the people around them catching cabs or walking down the street.

Just them, and the warm, soft pressure of Tyler's hand on his hip, and their lips together as they shared a moment of vulnerability.

Alec finally got a grip on himself and pulled back,

clearing his throat. "I mean… I keep trying to wait until my duty of care is…. over."

"Until I heal up?"

Alec nodded. "There aren't many other PTs I'd trust with your care, because I want to make sure everything is done right. I want you to be as well as possible. But… God. I was going to wait another couple weeks or a month or however long it is—"

"It better not be a month," Tyler interjected in a mutter, eyeing Alec sharply.

Alec sighed at him. He'd gone over this before. "Even when I let you get behind the wheel, you're not fully healed. You'll have to keep up with your recovery."

"Good."

Alec snorted with laughter. "Stubborn bastard."

"I think you like that about me." Tyler's cocky grin was back. "You were gonna wait, but you just can't. I'm that irresistible."

Alec shook his head, but he couldn't resist laughing. "You're *such* a prick."

"Speaking of things you like about me." Tyler was grinning like the cat who got the cream. "Only another week or two before I've healed enough for vigorous activity. Right, doc?"

"How long's your fucking Uber gonna take?" Alec shook his head, trying not to let Tyler win.

Tyler glanced at his phone and sighed. "It's right around the corner. Damn."

"Good. You can take that attitude right home with you."

"If I can't take you, it'll have to do." Tyler's hand found Alec's shoulder again, and he leaned in for another kiss. Despite his cocky words, it was gentle—tentative.

Alec welcomed it and closed his eyes for a moment to enjoy the warmth of Tyler's lips and the way his body seemed to align itself to Tyler's automatically. Like he was the center of the universe. And as far as he was concerned, he was. Alec pulled back, laughing to himself.

"What?" Tyler grinned.

"Nothing. Get home, you. I'll talk to you tomorrow about something." Alec spotted a black car pulling up with an Uber sticker in the window. "There's your car, I bet."

"Keeping me in suspense?" Tyler pouted. "Not very sportsmanlike."

"I can play dirty." Alec caught his breath when Tyler didn't say anything in response—just winked, turning his flirtation into an even deeper level of sexual innuendo. "Go on. Scram."

"Fine, fine. Don't say I don't follow my doctor's orders. See you soon," Tyler added, raising his hand in a little wave before he climbed into the car.

As he pulled away, Alec watched after him. It took him another few moments to remember he needed a cab of his own. Goddamn, Tyler made it hard to focus on anything.

Alec flagged down the nearest passing car and scrambled inside, unable to remember the last time he'd even taken one anywhere. He hardly remembered how—the driver had to prompt him for his home address.

Tyler was maddeningly right. Alec *was* attracted to his boisterous attitude and his unstoppable flirtatious nature, and even the small things: the way he handled the obvious pain without complaint, and the way he teased most of the time, but listened when Alec really needed him to.

One way or another, however stupid of an idea it was, he was going to have that man.

Fifteen

TYLER

Everything about this accident fucking sucked.

At least he could reach up now, if he did it slowly and carefully enough. Walk around, if he didn't mind limping. That was an improvement, right?

He itched with restless frustration as he shifted on the porch swing. The cushion was flat—not quite thick enough to protect his ass from the wood boards. At least this was a nice, easy place to sit and watch the comings and goings of the dude ranch guests.

The place was a neat little idea. Josh had taken off for a few years before coming back to Knoxville when his dad died and left him the farm. He hadn't wanted to run a ranch, but a small business development center loan and a summer of working his ass off had seen him convert it to a dude ranch. Now, instead of managing cattle, he managed honey-mooners, bachelor parties, wannabe-cowboys, and the occasional family of bored teens and fake-enthusiastic parents.

Tyler admired his entrepreneurial spirit. He was easily as outgoing as Josh, but he would have gone crazy trying to run the business side of things. He just liked driving fast cars and doing what the PR people told him to.

Which reminded him—he'd been keeping his head down on social media for the last couple days, but he wasn't gonna get away with that for long. According to Sarah, the threads on the internet were still… growing? Spinning? Whatever.

He and Alec hadn't had time to meet up since that night at the bar with his buddies. He'd been waiting for Friday night, but they'd been texting every day lately.

Just little stuff. *How was your day?* and *I saw this awesome Storage Wars episode* and *OMG I can't believe you watch Storage Wars* and *Desperate times call for desperate measures* kind of stuff.

Tyler's phone, which was balanced in his lap as he gently swung, went off again. He picked it up quickly, grinning at the text preview on the screen.

I'd offer to help with the desperation, but I think you're fishing for that.

Tyler typed back quickly.

So what if I am? We both still win ;)

The response made him catch his breath. *I was gonna come over and talk if you wanted me to. Would your buddy mind?*

He had no idea. He'd never brought hookups back to Josh's place while staying with him. Mostly because he was usually injured if he was staying with his friend instead of in his own place.

But Alec wasn't just a hookup. He was a friend. Kind of. For now.

And now I know why Facebook has that "it's complicated" option, he thought with a rueful sigh.

He stared at the screen for a few more moments, then shook his head. "Fuck it." If Josh didn't like sharing space for an evening, Tyler could deal with it later. Send him a fruit basket or a hot guy from Grindr or something. Assuming Josh even came back to the cabin before it was late and Alec had left.

If he left tonight.

No getting your hopes up, he warned himself. It seemed like they had a hell of a lot to talk about before Alec would commit to anything... well... long-term.

On the other hand, whenever they were together, there was a magnetic attraction that made it damn hard to keep his hands off Alec. They'd better talk fast.

As long as we can talk fast ;) he answered.

Deal :) Be there in 30?

Tyler grinned. He was already stewing in that mix of nerves and eager anticipation that he recognized from his job, but not much else. Hookups rarely affected him this much. It was something about seeing Alec.

Damn, crushes were annoyingly inconvenient. No way could he focus on anything else until Alec arrived.

So he just sat on the swing, slowly rocking and watching people pass by as afternoon faded into evening, and the crickets started their relentless hum.

Once he got past his impatience and his frustration with himself, it was weirdly nice to slow down for a while. It often felt like life was passing in a blur: by the time he spotted something good, it was in his rearview mirror.

Not this time, though. Not with Alec.

He spotted the car pulling into the guest parking lot and Alec stepping out, raising his hand carefully to wave. He didn't catch Alec's eye, so he texted.

Straight ahead 400 feet and you'll see me. Big log house behind the row of cabins.

The answer made him laugh: *What's 400 ft? Damn it Jim, I'm a PT not an engineer.*

I'm watching you. I'll let you know if you've gone too far ;)

Creepy but oddly arousing.

This time, Tyler did crack up. At least laughing was a little less painful now, even if it wasn't exactly comfortable.

Alec spotted the path to the house and glanced up, then grinned and gave him a thumbs-up. He briefly disappeared around the side of the cabins before reappearing again as he headed up for the porch. "Hey!"

"You made it!" Tyler eased himself to his feet, careful to hide the exertion it took behind a broad grin.

Alec beamed back at him. "I'm coming up, so you better get this party started." God, he was gorgeous when he smiled like this—like he only saw Tyler, and none of the rest of the world mattered. He bounded up the two porch stairs with an ease and grace that Tyler envied.

I'll get back there soon, Tyler reminded himself. Injury was just a temporary setback. "Really?"

"You bet."

Tyler laughed as he met Alec at the top of the steps. For a moment, he wanted to lean in and kiss him, but then he remembered where they were.

"Nice place," Alec said, turning to look at the Main Street of the ranch. It ran from end to end, with small guest cabins dotted along it. A small store was set near the middle, which operated in limited hours to sell vacationers essentials like shampoo, penis and boob-shaped straws, and huge lube bottles.

Josh had been complaining lately about slow business, and it occurred to Tyler right then what the problem is. "Identity crisis."

"A good place to come when you have one?" Alec grinned. "I noticed the red convertible in the parking lot. Oh—I hope that's not yours."

Tyler laughed. "No way, man. Gimme ten years before I hit that phase."

"Can't wait to see what you pick," Alec teased. His gaze was searching, though. It was clear as daylight to Tyler what he meant: *I want to be around in ten years. Will you let me?*

"Yeah," Tyler murmured. He gave Alec a warm smile. "If you're not bored by then."

"Trust me. This is the most excitement I've had in… years." Alec nodded at the porch swing. "Wanna sit?"

"Nah," Tyler gestured inside instead. "We can get drinks." Plus, inside would be more private. He didn't want listening ears getting in on this.

Alec raised his brows, then nodded. "Is your buddy home?"

"He runs this place. He's usually out late. Sometimes he comes back at supper." Tyler checked his watch, then pushed the porch door open and led Alec inside. "But it's past suppertime now."

Alec hummed. "So, all alone. However will we entertain ourselves?" His eyes sparkled as he closed the door after himself, then kicked his shoes off.

"I can think of a few ways," Tyler told him, smirking at the way Alec immediately blushed. "I'll put a sock on the knob."

Alec shielded his junk with a hand and grinned. "No, sir. Remember what we said?"

Tyler searched his memory. "Which one? The one where I warned you about being so goddamn hot?"

"Where we agreed that this is a bad idea." Alec's smile was wistful. "But I…"

He what? Tyler thought. *He wants me anyway? He can't wait and he's found someone else? He isn't into guys with my kind of lifestyle?*

"God, I need a beer."

Tyler was startled into a laugh. "Yeah. Me, too." He headed for the fridge and grabbed a couple cans, prying his open and sliding the other across the kitchen island to Alec.

For now, he kept the island between them. Maybe it would be enough distance to keep him from climbing Alec like a tree. A sexy little tree. Taller than him, but much less broad. The perfect size for an inner spoon.

Alec was snapping his fingers, grinning. "Earth to Tyler."

"Uh." Tyler's cheeks burned as he gulped beer. *Good job, genius.*

"I was about to admit that I can't keep my hands off you, but I think your brain got there first." Alec grinned, fidgeting with his beer can as he leaned on the other side of the island.

Tyler nodded. "Yeah. So, what do we do?"

Alec blinked. "Do?"

"I mean, do we keep pretending we're not crazy into each other?" Tyler smiled when that made Alec momentarily shy. It was that adorable expression when he stared at the ground instead of Tyler, his cheeks dimpling. "I'm serious, though. And it's not just sex, is it?"

"If it were, I wouldn't be here." Alec shook his head. "I've never not been able to walk away from a guy before." Then he looked sheepish. "Well, that's not strictly true. I fall over myself for sex. But *then* I walk away."

"The sex was that good, huh?" Tyler's ego swelled.

Alec laughed, and those brown eyes sparkled beautifully

as he tipped head back for a moment, exposing this throat. The sexy lump bobbed as he swallowed, and Tyler's gaze lingered at the base of his throat. He wished he could kiss it. "Oh, shut up," Alec finally told him, meeting his gaze again.

Tyler waggled his brows. "I'm taking it as a compliment, whatever you say."

"Take it however you want."

"Bent over the counter?" Tyler hummed. "I could be into that."

Alec blindly groped the counter for something to throw at him as he laughed. He found a packet of tissues and tossed it at Tyler, but it didn't even clear the counter surface.

Tyler laughed even harder. "Oh my God. That better not be your throwing arm. Aren't you a sporty guy?"

"I'm not sporty," Alec grumbled. "I deal with sporty guys. That doesn't automatically make me sporty. Like you're not a car."

"But I *am* fun to ride..." Tyler started, then saw Alec eyeing him sternly and raised his hands. "Okay! Serious talk. Let's get it over with." He surrendered to it. It was about damn time they got everything on the table anyway.

"When we were talking with your friends the other night," Alec said, "you sounded kind of like..." He drummed his nails on the counter in a staccato, rapid rhythm, like he was nervous. "You want to come out. And I'd already been thinking of... well, us."

"Spit it out," Tyler said, waiting for Alec to finish dancing around the point.

Alec said something that sounded a lot like "*Wanna GoPro me but I'm in only if yawn we could chestnut and sex,*" and then grabbed his beer can so hard it crumpled.

Tyler tried to parse that into English. "Wanna go..."

Alec clapped a hand over his mouth, looking mortified. "Oh, Jesus. I haven't done this in so long. You wanna... go to the opera?" he repeated, slower this time. "With me. If you want. I mean. We could just... not. We could just have sex. And be sex... partners..." he trailed off, his voice a mumble.

"And you said the sex wasn't good," Tyler smirked.

"I never said that! Dude. If you keep making fun of me, I *will* throw that tissue packet again. And I'll get it right between the eyes." Alec looked embarrassed as hell, but he was squarely meeting Tyler's gaze.

Tyler grinned at him. "Good. Better than getting it in the eye. That stings."

This time, Alec did come around the counter after him, and Tyler found the surprisingly strong guy's hands tickling his sides.

"Oh, fuck!" It was Tyler's turn to be embarrassed as his voice squeaked and he tried to squirm away. Sensation danced and jumped across his skin, making him thrash in Alec's hold. "Okay okay okay stop dude, I'll stop!" he begged.

When Alec stopped tickling him, he kept his arms around Tyler's waist, holding him upright until he had his balance again. Which was just enough time to notice that Alec was half-hard, even if he seemed to be trying to keep his hips angled away from Tyler's ass.

Too late. Tyler smirked and pressed back into Alec, grinding against him slowly. He pressed his hands over Alec's on his waist, making sure Alec kept holding him. "Hello, there," he murmured.

Alec cut his moan off, but he didn't let go of Tyler. His breathing was close now, his mouth next to Tyler's ear. It was quick and shallow now. "Hey."

Did Alec feel the same way that Tyler did every time they

touched? The same electric shocks of desire and need, mixed with something stranger and less familiar? *Rightness.* That was it.

"You feel that too, huh?" Tyler murmured.

Alec chuckled quietly, propping his chin on Tyler's shoulder. "Wanting to fuck you? Obviously."

Tyler closed his eyes for a moment, just breathing in the scent of him. He was always fresh and breezy. Like he'd just been hung on a laundry line. The mental image made him fight back a laugh.

"What?" Alec murmured.

Tyler shook his head. "I just… yeah. Yeah, I want to go to the opera with you. But I'm totally the wrong guy to choose."

"Why's that?"

Tyler had expected Alec to reject the idea and reassure him that he was going to be just fine there, not ask *why*. He fumbled for a moment, trying to explain it. "I… I'm not that guy. I mean, I don't know anything about it."

"So? I don't know anything about racing. Well, hardly anything. All I know is the physical problems it tends to encourage in drivers' bodies, and what muscles you need to strengthen to manage it."

"That's work, though," Tyler shook his head. He felt strangely vulnerable all of a sudden, but Alec's hold around him was firm and soothing. "I'm not… I'm just a dumbass who drives fast cars and sometimes crashes them. That's not boyfriend material."

"I think," Alec murmured, shifting his chin off Tyler's shoulder and leaning around to kiss his cheek, "that you're caught up in the image of what a driver should be. Which keeps you wanting to get back to the track early. Keeps you thinking you're supposed to act straight. Keeps you thinking you're stupid. You're really not."

Tyler's cheeks burned, and he turned his face away from Alec's, his jaw tightening.

Footsteps echoed on the porch outside.

They jumped apart like an electric car off the start line. In a second, they were a friendly distance apart, Alec striding around the other side of the counter.

And Tyler felt a weird ache that he never had before at the idea that they needed to hide this.

Shit. Oh, shit. He's right.

"Hey, Ty—Oh." Josh looked startled for a moment at the sight of Alec. "Oh, you must be Alec." He was starting to grin now.

Tyler's cheeks flushed defensively. "Yeah," he answered. "What's up?"

"Just making sure you didn't fall over and break a hip, old man." Josh punched Tyler's shoulder lightly on the way to the fridge, then reached out to shake Alec's hand. "Hey, I'm Josh."

"Hey. Alec."

"Good to meet you at last. The guys mentioned you," Josh added, grinning again at Tyler.

Oh, come on. Fuck off. Josh couldn't have known he was interrupting an important moment, but Tyler was no less pissed off about it. He gave Josh a pointed look.

"Okaaay, I'll be out late tonight. Got a bunch of stuff to take care of down at the office." Josh grabbed a sandwich, a bag of grapes, and a couple cans of beer. "See you."

He breezed out of there a minute later, and stillness settled again over them both.

Alec laughed lightly. "He seems a lot like you."

"A whirlwind of optimistic joy?" Tyler snorted with

amusement. "Yeah. We're pretty much best buddies. Have been for a long time. The other guys are all good friends, too, but I spend the most time around him, and this place."

"Yeah. I can tell."

It hadn't always been that way. Josh had barely had Tyler over when he was a kid. A working farm wasn't a great place to hang out as a teen, and Tyler had always assumed Josh thought it was uncool. They'd spent way more hours hanging out in the basement of Tyler's parents' house, playing video games and swapping tales about the guys they'd bang if they had the chance.

Now, though, the farm was Josh's own. It was very different here. It felt like a cozy little refuge from the world. Tyler worried that Josh was using it as exactly that—shutting out relationships—but he'd never had a leg to stand on in telling him that.

Not until now, anyway.

He drew a breath and looked back at Alec, then offered a smile. "So, yeah. I have a bunch of bullshit ideas about who I am, and... well. Some of them are kinda true. I mean, dating me—I'm gone ten months out of the year. I only get back for a weekend here and there, especially in the summer. Even if race day is Saturday, a lot of the time, I'll get there on Tuesday while they're building the car. You know?"

Alec nodded seriously. "Beats a boyfriend who's gone three hundred and sixty-five days a year." When Tyler gave him a puzzled look, he grinned and added, "Who doesn't exist."

"Oh." Tyler snorted with amusement. "I'm glad I beat *nobody*. Or the six-foot-tall invisible boyfriend."

"No. That's not what I meant," Alec said, stepping around the counter again and approaching him. "I mean... I'd rather be alone than with someone for the sake of it, or I would have started dating losers years ago. I wanted to wait until I found someone I can be me with." He gripped Tyler's hands. "We don't know if this will work out, but we don't have to know that to give it a shot."

Tyler couldn't deflect that one with a joke. His cheeks flushed, and then he slowly nodded. "What about your job?"

Alec scoffed. "Yeah. I've let that hold me back until now. But I also know I don't want a life where all I do is go to work in the morning, and come home, and eat supper alone, and watch TV for an hour or two, and then repeat that... for the rest of my life." His voice choked up, and he cleared his throat.

God. Tyler had always thought of office jobs as boring, but with the tight-knit circle of friends who had surrounded him since high school, he'd never thought about what life would be like without them.

He was always surrounded by a team of world-class experts in mechanics, engineering, marketing, and driving. Even in the car, he had a spotter there in his ear the whole time.

Alec's loneliness was impossible for him to mask, and it tugged at something within Tyler that he hadn't really noticed before.

Yeah, he was lonely, too. In his own way. Maybe not as alone, physically, but when he watched Deen with Nico, or Blane with Falcon, or Roman with Oscar, and now even Dustin with Leo... well, he and Josh were the only ones left.

He could joke around with Josh, but there was nobody who held him and told him exactly what was wrong like Alec did, and loved him anyway.

And just like he believed his body could heal when Alec

told him so, he was starting to think that he could *become* the boyfriend Alec deserved. Maybe not with the perfect schedule like all his friends seemed to have now, but someone who was enough for Alec.

"I… I wanna try. If you won't get in trouble with your professional… thingies," Tyler gestured. "Organization, or whatever."

"I have favors to call in here and there." Alec looked serious. "I'll refer you to someone else who specializes in the field. With a high-profile case *and* my personal recommendation, it's no problem."

Tyler's chest ached for a moment at the thought of giving up Alec's care—but Alec was right. It was for the best. And he could always tell Alec what the other guy said, and get a second unofficial opinion from him.

Before this, he'd been to a dozen physical therapists in his career. He'd turned out fine after each one. This wasn't an obscure specialty or anything. And Alec's career would be safe.

"I'll miss you," Tyler murmured, his gaze dropping.

Alec laughed. "Oh, don't give me those eyes. This means we can see each other *more*, Ty."

"Fine, fine," Tyler grumbled, picking up his nearly-empty can. He swigged the last few gulps of beer and set it aside, then poked Alec in the chest. "But I'm just about healed anyway. I wanna show you."

"How—" Alec started, and then his eyes narrowed suspiciously. "It better not be wall sex."

"Damn." Tyler pulled an even sadder face.

"Oh, God help me," Alec grumbled. "*Able* to drive doesn't equal *should* lift one-sixty, even with a wall for support!"

Just seeing that grumpy expression made Tyler crack up.

"Joking. Get your sexy ass to the bedroom before I make good on that countertop idea."

For a second, Alec looked like he was considering it. Then he finished his own beer and grinned, sauntering past Tyler to the bedroom. "I guess we'll have to save that for my place, where privacy is guaranteed."

"Something to look forward to," Tyler growled, swatting Alec's sexy little ass.

His boyfriend? No, not quite. Not officially, right? He wasn't gonna ruin the mood by asking just yet.

One more forbidden fling and they could bring this into broad daylight.

The thought was kind of hot. Being able to hold Alec's hand in public, or talk about him to the team, or see him in the VIP section after a race…

This might not be the worst thing ever.

CHAPTER
Sixteen

TYLER

THEY TUMBLED THROUGH THE GUEST ROOM DOOR TOGETHER, laughing giddily. Somehow, they'd wound up roughhousing their way down the hallway when Alec asked him which way the guest room was.

Tyler barely steered Alec inside before he shut the door behind them and pushed Alec up against it.

Alec's breathing was quick, his pupils wide as he stared at Tyler. "You *are* healing. I still don't know if it's enough for this..."

"If you're thinking clearly enough to go into doctor mode, I'm not doing my job yet," Tyler muttered, leaning in to kiss Alec thoroughly.

By the time he pulled away, his lips tingled with the taste and feeling of Alec against him, and his body had somehow pushed up against Alec's of its own accord. He was grinding against Alec in slow thrusts of his hips.

Honestly, he wasn't sure how he was gonna manage this. He couldn't really pick the guy up, for all his bluster and bravado. Crouching over him was a no-go. Missionary? Holding himself up on his arms was still a problem.

There *was* one solution.

"I wasn't kidding," Tyler growled. "I want to see you ride me again."

Alec didn't even stop to question it. He moaned, his hard cock pressing into Tyler's hip. "Yes," he panted. He arched away from the door, wrapping his arms around Tyler's back. "I want you."

Those three words ignited the fire of energy that had slowly been building up under Tyler's skin. Being forced to sit around doing nothing, not even hooking up with random guys to take the pressure off, had left him stewing for this.

He *needed* Alec so badly it hurt.

"Come," he ordered, backing away from Alec and toward the bed.

As he hit the bed, lowering himself onto it as gently as he could, Tyler stripped his jeans. It only took a little creative maneuvering to get them off with a minimum of aching, and Alec was busy stripping.

God, Alec was gorgeous. Slender but muscled, his pecs catching Tyler's eyes first. Then he looked up to admire those gorgeous eyes, the scruff along his cheeks, and down to admire... well, the obvious.

Tyler's cock was thick and straight.

"Climb up," Tyler told him.

Alec didn't hesitate to obey him, which would be very convenient for keeping him from worrying about Tyler's recovery and killing the mood... or worse yet, telling the other physical therapist to keep him off the track for even longer than this one last week Tyler was gonna have to endure.

Tyler was happy to boss Alec around if the end result was hot sex, a boyfriend he could be open about, *and* getting back into the racing game.

He grinned, his mood soaring as Alec straddled his shoulders and braced himself on the headboard. "That's it," he encouraged, gazing up Alec's body to make eye contact. "You don't like my smart mouth? Fuck it," he breathed. "Shut me up."

Alec laughed, cupping his cheek for a moment. His thumb rubbed along Tyler's jaw, and then over his lip. His smile faded into a mesmerized stare as Tyler darted his tongue out to lick Alec's thumb suggestively.

Then Alec gripped himself, sliding the head of his cock across Tyler's lips. "Are you sure?"

"I'm not telling you twice," Tyler growled. "If you wanna be in charge, you'll have to come up with a better ide—nigh!"

Alec started to push himself inside, and Tyler sucked his cheeks around the thick length.

God, he loved sucking Alec's dick. The taste of him was irresistible enough to turn Tyler on, let alone the sight of him crouched over Tyler, holding himself upright as he thrust slowly into Tyler's mouth.

Tyler circled his tongue around the head whenever Alec pulled back enough to let him, and sucked the shaft into the back of his throat when Alec pushed forward.

"Fuck," Alec panted, his grip shifting from Tyler's cheek to his shoulder. "Oh, man. You feel so good."

Tyler managed a groan in response around Alec's cock. His cock was begging for attention, too, so he slid his hand down his own body to tug gently on himself at first, then stroke harder. He tried to match the rhythm of Alec's thrusts, keeping it slow but tight.

God, it was good.

Just like the last time they'd fucked, this was going to the top of his shower jerk-off fantasies. Well, *memories*, not fantasies. That made it even better.

"I want to ride you now," Alec moaned, shifting his weight to one leg and swinging the other over Tyler's chest to dismount and rummage through the bedside table. "Got lube?"

Tyler stole the chance to smack that sexy ass and grinned at the startled noise Alec made. "Top drawer."

"Oh. Duh." Alec managed to pull it out, his motions fumbling and clumsy.

God, seeing him so turned-on he lost his usual graceful coordination was hot in itself. Tyler grinned, continuing to stroke himself slowly as he watched Alec slick his fingers.

Alec crouched over his legs, gently pushing them together so he could spread his knees and brace himself on one hand and both knees. His free hand slid between his legs, two fingers disappearing behind his balls.

Tyler didn't need to see the show to tell when Alec had slid those fingers inside himself. Alec tensed up and gasped, then moaned breathily, his fingers tightening in the sheets.

Fuck, that was hot. Picturing himself inside Alec was even better, and it was all he could do not to stroke himself harder and faster. He wanted to hold out as long as he could for him.

"I could watch you jerk off all day," Alec whispered. His gaze had shifted from eye contact to staring at Tyler instead.

Tyler grinned and slowed his motions, rubbing his hand around the tip of his cock. He thrust his hips upward a few times, fucking his fist so the head of his rock-hard shaft appeared from the circle of his thumb and forefinger.

"I'm good," Alec gasped, pulling his hand away from himself and grabbing a condom.

Tyler laughed at his impatience. "Are you sure?"

"I'm fucking ready," Alec told him sharply, knocking Tyler's hand away and rolling the condom on. Then, he ran his slick fingers down Tyler's shaft and shifted his body into position.

God, the pressure of Alec's hole against the tip of him was divine. Alec ground slowly, teasing them both with it before he got started.

Alec looked at Tyler, a smile dancing around his lips.

"What?" Tyler grinned.

"I… I daydreamed a lot about this lately," Alec admitted, laughing softly. "It's just surreal."

"You can make it real," Tyler murmured, resting his hands on Alec's thighs.

"If I'd known all it took was opera tickets…" Alec shook his head.

Tyler laughed, carefully raising his hand to cup Alec's cheek. That hint of a smartass in him was incredibly attractive. "Just fuck me… fuck yourself on me… whatever."

"Oh, I'll fuck you," Alec promised, grinning down at him.

Suddenly, Tyler wasn't so sure he was in charge after all. And just as suddenly, he was fine with that.

"Go on, then," Tyler dared him, grinning. "Double-dog dare you."

The noise Alec made as he sank onto Tyler's cock was a mix of a laugh and a groan. "Oh, God."

"Was that for me or my dick?"

"Both."

"Again, taking it as a compliment." Tyler kept his hands

on Alec's thighs and out of the way as Alec gripped him firmly, enveloping him slowly.

It was just as incredible as last time, even if the desire to flip Alec over and go to town was even stronger. Being forced to slow down and let Alec take over was probably good for him—spiritually or something—but it made him grind his teeth.

"You all right?" Alec murmured, his gaze flickering up to Tyler's. Damn, he was observant.

"Fine," Tyler whispered, offering him a quick grin. "Just want you, baby."

Alec's smile wavered, but he seemed to find in Tyler's face whatever he was looking for, because it grew to a grin. "Yeah. It's been too fucking long."

"Yeah. Two weeks is too long now."

Tyler wasn't even joking; he'd felt the need building up like an itch he couldn't scratch—of which he also had plenty lately. Still, Alec rolled his eyes. "Don't make me gag you."

"Shame you can't do it with your cock while you're riding m—hnngh!" Alec pressed his hand across Tyler's mouth, preventing him from finishing that sentence.

Okay, that was *really* hot.

"I think you like a guy who can shut you up," Alec whispered, his eyes sparkling mischievously.

Tyler's cheeks burned as his body flooded with adrenaline and… something pleasurable. He had no idea what this was, but it was suddenly the hottest sex he'd ever had.

His hips bucked involuntarily to thrust deeper into Alec, and Alec shifted his weight to press his other hand on Tyler's stomach, pushing him down. "No. Not until I say so."

Tyler bit back his whimper. He was suddenly hyperaware of every touch of skin on skin, like Alec was electrically charged. Discovering this whole new side of himself was fiery bliss.

"If you want me to stop, just... I dunno, bite me."

Tyler tried to laugh, but it was hard behind Alec's hand. He nodded slightly, maintaining eye contact as Alec started moving again.

Alec took Tyler in short, sharp jerks of his hips. Every thrust wrapped Tyler's cock in tight, warm, heavenly heat. Before long, Alec had a rhythm and his focus slipped. He tipped his head back, groaning in pleasure, and then looked back at Tyler. Watching the sheen form across his smooth skin and the way his expression screwed up in pleasure was incredibly erotic.

Now he wasn't shy, and it was hot as hell.

When Tyler couldn't make smartass comments, it was strangely quiet, which only deepened the bond between them. He couldn't shake the feeling that they were sharing an experience that was more than it seemed.

"Your cock feels incredible inside me," Alec whispered, breaking the silence. "I want to make you come in me someday. I wanna feel you, hot and wet, pulsing inside me..."

Tyler's sound was stifled, but he nodded his head quickly. *God, yes. I needed to get tested anyway. I'm gonna go, like, tomorrow.*

"I'll let you tell me what you want later," Alec added, giving him that mischievous wink again. "And I'll consider any requests."

Tyler bit his lip, gasping against Alec's palm as he pressed his head back into the pillow.

Alec hadn't stopped for a second, and the pleasure was building up deep in his stomach. He wasn't gonna last much longer. Especially with the way Alec's hand ran up and down his torso, rubbing across the muscles Tyler had worked so hard to develop, since he had nothing better to do with his time.

Not until he'd met Alec, anyway. Now, he wasn't so sure.

Alec tweaked his nipple and Tyler just about arched off the bed with the mix of pain and pleasure that zinged through him. *Fuck*, that felt good in a way he couldn't describe. It ignited nerves that seemed to shoot straight down to his cock, making him clench and twitch.

"Oh, I felt that," Alec whispered. "You liked it, huh?" He flicked his fingers gently across the sensitive nub, then rubbed them in a slow circle.

Tyler nodded, closing his eyes for a few seconds as he moaned into Alec's hand. He needed more stimulation, and he needed it right the fuck now.

Luckily, so did Alec. He shifted his hand to Tyler's shoulder and gripped firmly, speeding up the pace at which he pushed himself down onto Tyler's throbbing, sensitive shaft. "Oh, I'm gonna come on you, baby," he whispered. "Maybe even hands-free. You hit just the right spot in me."

Tyler tipped his head down, gazing past Alec's arm to his cock, bobbing in the air between them with every thrust of their bodies. God, watching himself disappear inside Alec was so hot.

"I'm gonna come," he tried to mumble, but the sounds blurred into indistinct syllables.

Alec read his expression, though. "You're close, aren't you, baby? Just let me come. I'm gonna come. Any moment now," he gasped, his hips shuddering as he lost the rhythm and desperately plunged their bodies together.

Just as Tyler was about to try to wrestle for control, Alec gasped, shutting his eyes and rolling his head back. "Ty!"

A single syllable, but the way it rolled off Alec's tongue—in pleasure and desperate need, sweeping through Alec's body—was… memorable was an understatement. He'd heard his name gasped by lovers before, of course, but not like this.

Alec pulsated around Tyler, his sticky mess spraying freely across Tyler's stomach and the sheets. His thrusts slowed as he came, gasping and moaning for breath. "Ah… ah, that's amazing. Fuck," he whispered, finally stopping.

Tyler was so close it almost hurt. Just a little more would do it. He was clinging to the edge, desperate for a hand—or desperate to plunge over the edge, he wasn't sure which.

Which was a lot like him and Alec right now, in the bigger picture, but he had time to think about that later.

Tyler gripped Alec's hips and thrust into him a few times, and suddenly Alec pulled his hand away from Tyler's lips.

Alec was kissing him deeply, so when Tyler couldn't hold back a second longer and gasped Alec's name, it was against those beautiful lips.

Alec held him close, stroking his shoulders and cheeks and rubbing the back of his neck while Tyler thrust into him, letting ecstasy consume him. Tyler braced himself on one elbow, holding Alec's lower back with the other hand.

Sharp pain returned to his ribs the moment the peak of orgasm had passed, which reminded him why he was supposed to be letting Alec take over. He collapsed flat against the bed, trying to catch his breath.

"Fucking… fuck," Tyler mumbled, blinking a few times as he stared up at Alec.

"Agreed." Alec was sweaty and out of breath, but grinning at him like they shared a secret.

Which they did—for now.

Tyler ignored the warning twangs of pain as he reached

up to cup Alec's cheek, rubbing slowly with his thumb. "That was… wow."

"You *do* like me taking over." Alec gave him a broad grin.

"And you *are* a bossy little twerp." Tyler made a mock *tsch* sound.

"And…" Alec pretended to think. "If I remember right, about thirty seconds ago, it made you come so hard you just about lost your damn mind."

Tyler couldn't argue that. He laughed breathlessly, his hand unconsciously going to his ribs. "Fuck off."

"I'm right and you know it."

Alec had figured out the key to Tyler's heart, somehow. The next question was so obvious he didn't even think twice before asking it. "You staying the night?"

Alec hesitated for a second, then nodded. "If you're inviting me."

"I am." Tyler shifted awkwardly as Alec rolled off him so he could pull off the condom and grab tissues.

"Then," Alec murmured, kissing his cheek and handing over the tissue box, "I will."

"Good." Tyler wrapped his arm around Alec and pulled him into his side. "This mean we're boyfriends?"

That shyness was back, and Alec ducked his head. "Again, if you're asking."

"I am."

"Then yeah." Alec pressed his lips against Tyler's shoulder and slid his hand gently across his ribs to rest on his other side.

"Good." Tyler grinned. "That's my mission for the day done. By the way, I already added you to my VIP list. You can get in anywhere I'm driving, anytime, free. If you want to."

"If you're asking," Alec murmured.

Tyler chuckled. "I am," he said for the third time.

Alec chuckled, the sound mellow and sleepy. He didn't answer, but he pressed his cheek into Tyler's shoulder.

Bliss seeped through Tyler's very bones, warming him gently from head to toe. That feeling was back: the feeling of rightness.

"Good?" Alec murmured, just as sleep tugged on Tyler's consciousness.

Tyler just managed a quiet, "Yeah. I am. You?"

Alec didn't seem prone to hyperbole, so when he murmured, "I really, really am," Tyler's pride swelled like never before.

This would never work out, but goddamn, he was glad he'd gotten to experience this at least once.

CHAPTER
Seventeen

ALEC

ALEC COULDN'T SHAKE THE FEELING THAT HE SHOULD HAVE heard from Tyler by now.

A morning phone call to Doc Gordon, one of the few guys who dealt with even more guys from the racing world than Alec did, had put Tyler on his patient roster for Wednesday.

He hadn't exactly said *why* he needed someone else to take over the case, but Dr. Gordon had been more than happy to do it. From what Alec had heard, he'd worked with a few of the biggest names over the last decade, so Tyler's team management ought to have been happy, too.

Everyone won, right? So why hadn't Tyler let him know how the appointment went?

It was in Nashville, so he'd given Tyler a few hours to get home—then a few more. Alec's office was closed for the day, so Tyler was definitely back by now, but... still nothing.

He hadn't realized how the hours dragged by until now, but his usual routine of coming home and turning on the TV just didn't cut it anymore. Especially when he was waiting to hear back from his brand-new boyfriend.

As the street lamps flickered on and the sun set, there was no word. "Come on, man," he mumbled, poking his phone screen for what felt like the hundredth time to make sure he hadn't missed anything.

But still no word.

Goddamn it. As his boring evening drew to a close, he finally concluded that he was just going to have to be patient. And maybe get out on that goddamn bike and do something with all this restless energy.

Not that Tyler was the center of Alec's life now, but he'd still heard nothing by Thursday afternoon, and it bothered him.

Sure, it wasn't unusual for them to go a day or two without texting, but having not heard from him since their Monday night together? It was a little weird.

Alec reminded himself that he probably had other commitments. Helping Josh around the farm, or maybe meeting with his family. He seemed like the type who had a loving family.

I'm not jealous, either, he told himself. And he almost believed it.

He'd bought himself a bike to distract himself, but then day after day passed and he hadn't yet tried it out for any longer a ride than around the block.

He kept his cool as best he could as the work day drew to a close, but Rosie had noticed something was off. She waited until the last patient had left and he'd locked up before flagging him down, mercifully.

"Where did the ants come from?"

"Is this like a *what did the fox say* thing?" Alec didn't keep up with memes as much as he could have, but he'd heard that song playing on Rosie's desktop way too much a few summers ago.

Rosie laughed. "In your pants."

"Ah." Alec checked the buttons on his shirt sleeves and tugged them down, avoiding her gaze as he shrugged his jacket off and hung it on the usual peg. He straightened it until it was just so.

"Boy problems," she surmised. "Boy*friend* problems? He didn't turn you down for the opera, did he?"

"No. No, he… well." Alec crinkled his nose, trying to think back to that conversation. "I *think* he accepted. We got a little distracted."

Rosie snickered. "I'll say! If you can't even remember if he said yes!"

Alec swatted at her and then fidgeted with his collar, suddenly embarrassed. Was that too unprofessional of him to have said?

Rosie waved a hand impatiently. "Well?"

"I, um… haven't heard from Ty since I referred him to Doc Gordon." Alec frowned.

"The one in Nashville?"

Alec nodded.

Rosie hummed, then glanced at the clock. "If I hurry, I might get through to reception and see if he attended."

"Oh, I know Ty attended. I sent the doctor an email thanking him and he said it was a pleasure to help." Alec shook his head. "God knows what he thinks of me passing him off to him…"

"What Doc Gordon thinks, or Ty?"

Rosie's question was more perceptive than Alec realized at first, as he opened his mouth to answer, then closed it again. "Oh. I guess I'm more worried about Tyler."

"That he thinks you don't want him anymore? Or you're worried he doesn't want you?"

Alec was dumbstruck for a few moments. He didn't really know how to answer, but his cheeks flushed with embarrassment. His eyes stung, but he blinked rapidly and shrugged as he checked his pockets for his car keys.

He knew he was running from the situation—from his own thoughts—but Rosie let him do it.

"Just something to think about. Don't let it slip away," Rosie told him. "And for God's sake, take off early tomorrow. The last couple hours are empty. Cancellations. I'll keep them free."

Alec shook his head slowly. "Why?"

"So you can go find out what's going on," Rosie told him patiently.

"Ah." Alec cleared his throat. The thought of driving up to the farm and finding Tyler there avoiding him... or not there...

"Call him first," Rosie told him. "Find out what's happening. Just talk about it, Alec. Like you would a professional problem. It's okay to talk about your feelings, too."

He got the feeling she was teasing him, but he couldn't be sure. He just nodded slowly. "Yeah, I guess. Okay, I'm taking off. See you tomorrow."

Rosie's advice played on his mind for the whole drive home. He'd already been thinking about it, but something had been stopping him.

Now he knew what: the fear of what Tyler's answer might be.

It was a hard one to wrap his mind around. It didn't make sense, but that didn't stop him feeling the fear.

"Just do it, man," he mumbled, tapping his steering wheel as he drove on autopilot. "The minute you get home. Don't put it off."

Three days without hearing from his brand-new boyfriend seemed like cause enough for a phone call. Hell, it was probably enough for a visit if Tyler didn't answer.

Just as he'd promised himself, when he walked in the door, he pulled out his phone and didn't let himself put off the call.

His stomach lurched when Tyler answered on the first ring. "Hey, it's Ty."

Alec hadn't expected that, so he fumbled for words for a few moments. "Ty—hey—um, hi. It's Alec."

"Aw, shit. I didn't text, did I?"

"Nope." Alec chuckled. "Been thinking you went and fell off a horse."

Tyler laughed. "I'm smart enough to stay away from things with a mind of their own, aside from cars. Sorry, though. I should have answered."

"Why? What's been going on?"

"Lots of work stuff," Tyler said vaguely. "And then the appointment in Nashville, of course."

"How was he?"

"He's… well, he's not you. But he was all right."

Alec smiled and sank onto the couch, stopping his pacing. "Yeah? What'd he say?"

Tyler laughed. "Same stuff as you, don't worry." His voice turned teasing as he added, "Or am I spying for you? PT espionage?"

"No," Alec snorted. "Silly."

"That I am."

There was an awkward pause for a few moments. Alec wished he'd dropped by now—it was impossible to read Tyler's body language. "So, uh. Can I see you this weekend?"

"How about next week?" Tyler hedged. "Like, Monday?"

"Aren't you going out with the guys Friday?"

"Oh, that's—that's not every Friday."

"I'm sure they said last time that next week—" Alec started, but Tyler interrupted.

"I mean, *I* don't go every Friday."

"Right, right. Monday works for me. The opera is Tuesday night anyway."

"Tuesday's a weird day for it. But I should be here—I mean, free that night."

Another pause while Alec furrowed his brows. Tyler wasn't thinking of racing again, was he? "You know, no matter what Doc Gordon said, you aren't fit to get back in the car that soon." Technically, Tyler probably *could* sit up for that long, but the heat was climbing and the physical exertion wasn't just in bursts—it was a constant grind around the track, around and around. He wasn't confident a healing body could handle that toll.

"Oh, I know my limits." Tyler sighed, but his voice softened. "I appreciate that you're worrying about me, though. That's... nice. New, but nice. I'm sorry I worried you by, um... vanishing."

Placated, Alec slowly relaxed. "Yeah. Don't do that again, or I'll drive over there and smack your pretty little ass."

Tyler's gulp was audible. "Uh huh. My... yeah. Uh huh." He sounded like he was short-circuiting, or perhaps in public. Maybe both.

"Oh, I'll definitely smack that ass if you want me to," Alec teased to lighten the mood. "Just say the word."

"I'm so in public right now, dude," Tyler mumbled.

"Sucks to be you."

Tyler burst out laughing. "I... I like you. Even if you're a dick."

"I like you too, you dick," Alec said and laughed again.

The weirdness had smoothed out. He could figure out what the hell all that was about soon, but for now, they were talking.

"Talk to you soon, huh, babe?" Tyler asked. "I'll call this weekend and catch up."

"Yeah, please do. I like hearing from you." Alec missed seeing him in person, but Tyler did have other responsibilities. Unlike Alec, he had a family and friends and... maybe hobbies?

Alec would have to ask sometime. But not until he picked up hobbies of his own, or the conversation would be awkward when it turned to him. Which just got him thinking about his own life again, and he really didn't want that.

"I will, then," Tyler promised. "Hopefully I'll have great news."

"Oh?"

"I'm working on it." Tyler sounded like he was up to no good. "More on that soon."

"Good luck with it," Alec wished him. He couldn't think of what it might be, except... maybe investigating the crash. That could get dangerous, if someone seriously did wish him harm. "Be careful."

"I will. Thanks. Bye, hon."

"Bye," Alec bade, smiling at the pet name.

He felt a million times better upon hanging up, but it only took a few minutes for doubt to creep back in.

What was Tyler up to?

Eighteen

TYLER

"HOLY SHIT, MAN. YOU MADE IT!"

Tyler raised his hand in a careful wave as he strode up to the all-too-familiar car. His baby looked like she was ready to go this weekend, and not a moment too soon.

"Hey, Chess," he greeted his teammate with a manly hug, ignoring the wave of pain that nearly buckled his knees when Chess slapped his back.

"Shit, you should sit down. How are you doing?" He found himself ushered to the edge of the tent as the other guys waved to him and elbowed each other. Roger would be here any minute now, as word came on the grapevine that Ty had shown up to race.

"I'm all right," Tyler told Chess with a trademark grin. "They can't keep me down for long."

"Thought you'd be out for a lot longer, the way you got smashed up."

"Nah, man." Tyler shook his head. "I'll crawl out of my skin if they make me sit around doing nothing any longer."

Chess eyed him. "Are you seriously good for today? You know Roger's gonna grill you."

"Yeah, yeah. I know. I'm good. I know what I can do. I drove here," Tyler shrugged with his better shoulder.

"At seventy, maybe. How's one-fifty gonna treat you?"

Tyler knew he was in for a hell of a ride. He couldn't take the good drugs, either, so it was gonna be an endurance test. But he'd be damned if he was gonna sit around and let people coddle him when he was capable of doing the job. That just wasn't the kind of guy he was.

"I can sit, I can push pedals, and I can move my arms. That's all I gotta do."

Roger greeted him with, "Dead man walking! Jesus, it's good to see you again."

Tyler stood and turned to the tent entrance, squinting as Roger strode in. "Hey, Roger. Yeah, it's so good to be back." Once more, his ribs had to endure a crushing manly hug, and he hid his grimace in a grin when they pulled apart. "I'm ready to go."

"The doc check you out?"

"Transferred me to Doc Gordon out in Nashville. Gordon said he wouldn't stop me," Tyler grinned. Technically, he was bending the truth a little, but luck was on his side and Roger didn't question him about it.

"That's one thing," Roger said, squinting at him. "You sure *you're* up for it? Just 'cause Gordon says it…"

"I'm ready. Dude, missing one week killed me."

"As long as *not* missing one more won't really kill you this time," Roger told him.

That reminded Tyler—he had to talk to Roger about his suspicions. Richie had behaved himself during the last race, but there was no guarantee he wouldn't try the same stunt again this time.

"Can I have a word?"

As if summoned by his very thoughts, Richie passed by the tent and stopped short. His jaw dropped before he managed a grunted, "Hey. You're back."

Tyler jerked his chin in acknowledgment. "Can't keep me down."

He noticed the subtle downturn of Richie's lips. "Right. Cool. Good luck today."

Roger snorted with laughter. "He was glad not to see you last week. You gonna give him hell today?"

"Hell, yeah. That's what I wanted to mention, actually."

Movement by the fence caught his eye, and he spotted Richie. He'd gone straight over to talk to reporters.

That made Tyler uneasy.

Roger followed his gaze. "You think he sabotaged you, don't you?"

"I… I think so. I can't prove it. The investigation didn't turn up anything, did it?"

"Looked like a clean bump. No reason it should have ended…" Roger shivered. "Man, you had a close call."

Tyler glanced back at the car. Yeah, she was still his, but there were a hell of a lot of new parts on her. "I know."

"Sure you're ready for it? If he does have it out for you, he won't try the same stunt. But there's plenty of ways to skin a cat, or flip a car."

Tyler's jaw clenched. He wasn't gonna let one asshole ruin everything for him. "Isn't there anything we can do?"

"Heads up," Roger answered, nodding toward the tent entrance.

Shit. There was a team of reporters—a guy with a camera and someone carrying a microphone.

No doubt Richie had tipped them off to Ty's return to glory. Or…

I still haven't confirmed the rumors. "You think they're gonna…"

"Turn the conversation the way you want it to go. If you'd rather wait for Sarah to get involved…"

"No." Tyler was firm on that. He could handle this himself. It was the moment he'd been waiting for his entire career.

Just as Tyler expected, they didn't make it past thirty seconds of interview time—asking about his injuries, whether he was ready to get back in the car, what had happened on the track last time—before the question came up.

"While you were away, there were some rumors circulating about your, uh, relationship status."

Tyler smiled. "Yes."

"Is that confirming there's a—a man in the picture?"

"Yep." Tyler waited. Normally, the question would be about how they'd met, how the girlfriend in question felt about him racing, if she was a motorsports fan.

Instead, the question he got was, "How does it feel to be the first out gay man at your level in the league?"

Tyler raised his eyebrows. "Same as it feels to be the first out straight man, I imagine. I mean, none of us are thinking about wedding bells while we're behind the wheel."

Seemingly relieved at the answer, the reporter laughed, then moved on to ask him about his individual points record for the season, and whether he figured he'd be able to make up the absence.

That was it? Tyler fought back the confusion and even disappointment. He'd expected to be probed and questioned and maybe even given That Look. But they seemed happy to say as little as possible about it.

"What do you think your chances of winning today are?"

Tyler gave a broad grin. "I'm facing the winner's podium no matter what. You can flip me over but you can't keep me down."

The look on the reporter's face was priceless—he started to grin, froze, stared, then fumbled for words as he turned to the camera and finished the interview on autopilot.

The pair left without a word, and Tyler waited until they were just out of earshot before he cracked up.

The track was getting busier now. Every team had at least a dozen guys around, plus all the league employees, track employees, photographers, super-fans, and hangers-on.

With half an hour to go before his practice lap, he could afford to sit down for a minute. No sense in exhausting himself before the green flag.

As he sank into a camping chair to watch the guys arguing over his engine, Tyler stared at the front bumper, which was sitting next to the car right now in a pile of bolts and pieces.

What if…?

No way. The investigators would have checked, right?

Unless the bumper was so smashed up the evidence was gone.

A familiar voice reached Tyler's ears, and he drew a sharp breath.

"You look good in a fire suit."

It was Alec.

For a moment, Tyler couldn't make sense of it: what was he doing here of all places?

Then, the expression on Alec's face made Tyler pause. *Oh, shit.* He'd never seen Alec look pissed off before, but he was pretty sure this was what it looked like.

He was in trouble.

"Uh. Thanks."

Alec gave him a look that said *Really?*

"I mean, it'd be rude to turn down the compliment."

Sarah was at Alec's arm. She glanced between them, then raised her eyebrows. "This guy showed up, and he was on your comp list. I guess we're good?"

"Yeah," Alec answered for Tyler. "We're good."

Tyler opened his mouth, then closed it again and nodded once.

Sarah looked like she was trying not to laugh. "Good luck." She strode out of the tent.

Tyler could hear the sudden silence from the other guys. "C'mon. Let's take a walk."

"You're not walking an inch further than you have to. Sit down," Alec told him, his voice strangely friendly as he pulled up another camp chair. "We'll talk more after the race. You don't need any more pressure."

I'm fucked. Tyler nodded once. Alec was so gonna break up with him.

He had it coming anyway. He'd spent a few days moping after the appointment with Doc Gordon, and then he'd made his decision.

No more being babysat by Josh. No more being coddled by Alec. Tyler just wanted to race, and goddamn it, to prove he was still able to.

If Alec disagreed with the decision… well, Tyler could cry about it later. Right now, he had to do what had to be done.

"How's your range of motion?"

"Getting there. If I'm careful, I'll be okay."

"No sudden movements," Alec warned, his voice quiet. His hand rested on Tyler's, on the arm of his camp chair. "No sudden inhalation, either. You're not on anything, are you?"

Tyler shook his head.

"Good. If you're able to move around this much without medication, I'm impressed." Alec eyed him and added in an undertone, "And pissed off."

Tyler nodded. "Sorry…" he started, but Alec was shaking his head.

"Don't get into that yet. Now that I'm here, what can I do besides sit in the stands and watch you this evening?"

A smile crept across Tyler's face. Alec didn't hate him. He wasn't here to blow up and storm off. He was here to… to help?

It seemed too good to be true.

Tyler kept his voice so quiet that even Alec had to lean in. "Just tell me I can do this."

Alec's expression shifted from briskly professional to sympathetic. He squeezed Tyler's hand gently and murmured, "You better fucking do this. If you're willing to take this risk, you're gonna do it right."

"Yes, sir," Tyler murmured, offering a slight smile. "No fancy stunts today. Better to finish a little slow than not at all."

Alec nodded. "That's right. I've looked up videos of you, by the way. You've got talent."

Tyler tried not to blush, but it was futile. He could feel the guys sneaking glances at them. *Well, there's coming out, and then there's coming out.* "We still… uh, boyfriends?"

Alec's eyes crinkled in a slight smile, and then he puffed out a quick breath, shaking his head. Not in a *no* way, but in a *what an idiot* way. "Duh."

"Oh." Tyler's heart leapt, and he was suddenly smiling. "Cool."

"I'm not gonna break up with you the moment we start dating, as hard as you try."

A chuckle burst free as Tyler closed his eyes. His whole body was suddenly more relaxed, now that his mind was at ease. "Yeah. I did try pretty hard there, didn't I?"

"I'll still yell at you later if you like," Alec offered, grinning. "But I figured it might fray your concentration before your practice lap. Is that what they call it?"

Tyler's chest felt warm. "Yeah. That's what it's called, baby." It was so damn good to see Alec, and now that they were holding hands, he found himself unwilling to be the first one to let go.

"You'll have to head up to the stands soon—sorry."

Alec nodded. "I'll think very stable thoughts for you. Four on the floor, man."

Tyler burst out laughing, and then he leaned in to kiss Alec.

He didn't care who knew about them. He didn't even care who saw. Hell, he *wanted* them to see. He'd met just about everyone's girlfriends or wives before.

Finally—finally!—it was his turn.

For the first time in his life, winning on the track seemed less important than going home afterward. Although a win to impress Alec would be pretty damn sweet, too.

"Thank you," Tyler murmured, his gaze fixed on the ground.

Alec squeezed his hand gently. "You're welcome, you big damn idiot. Now, go kick that lap's ass."

Tyler beamed back at Alec and rose to his feet, slowly but steadily. "You know it, baby."

For the first time since the accident, Tyler's confidence was back to a hundred percent. He could do this—and he could do it well. And with Alec by his side, he was gonna figure out Richie's game and beat him at it, too.

God, it was good to be back.

Nineteen

ALEC

ALEC WAS GONNA FUCKING KILL HIS DUMBASS BOYFRIEND, BUT only after Tyler safely finished the race.

God, he hoped Tyler *did* safely finish.

If Tyler had decided he was ready—if Doc Gordon had said he was ready, despite Alec's advice—there was nothing anyone else could do about it.

And Alec had to figure out for himself whether his fears for Tyler's safety were going to be too big a problem.

This already felt so different from watching race day on TV. Not just because Tyler was *in* the race and not beside him on the couch.

The energy in the air from fans was incredible—and a little scary. He was in a separate section that looked like it was for VIPs, and it was filling up quickly now that the practice laps were over.

Pre-race commentators dotted the fence, and there was a personable announcer keeping a countdown to the green flag on the loudspeaker.

But Alec got the strong impression that some fans were there in the *hopes* of seeing a crash.

The nerves made his hands shake. Or maybe that was not eating since before he set out for the speedway from Josh's house.

Josh had been easy to find at the farm, and between them, they'd very quickly figured out what had happened. It sounded like it was Tyler's habit to get back to work quicker than he should have.

The announcer caught his attention briefly.

"Tyler Joseph is a surprise return to this race after the spectacular crash that kept him off the track for a few weeks. Hopefully he can keep his wheels on the ground today!"

His interest faded when the guys started talking about other car numbers. He only knew Tyler was 32, and that asshole Richie was in 67.

He caught a murmur from behind him. It sounded like a woman's voice. "Isn't Ty the one who came out online last week?"

"Yeah, I think so."

Alec froze, not daring to turn around yet. *Had* he? Or was it rumor? He really shouldn't say anything, but listening in felt weird when they didn't know who he was.

The first woman whistled. "He's got balls. I'd hate to be the first guy…"

"I know, huh? He's cute, though. Wonder if he's got a boyfriend."

"And a hundred women cried."

Alec turned halfway around, and the movement immediately attracted both of their attention.

One of them murmured, "Speaking of which."

The other one blushed and laughed as she leaned down. "Hey. Haven't seen you around here. Sponsor?"

"Me?" Alec laughed. "No. No, I'm a… uh, plus-one."

"Oh, friend?"

"Boyfriend."

"But there aren't…" It took one of them a few seconds of squinting at the track, then back at Alec. Then, she caught her breath. "Oh, my God. Sorry. Are you… I mean, do you and Tyler…"

"Yeah, I'm here for Ty."

"Hi! I'm Sally. Chess's girlfriend."

"And I'm Kiera. My husband's Ronnie. He's in number 45."

Alec recognized both names as teammates of Tyler's. Shit. He hadn't been prepared to meet the coworkers—or the coworkers' families.

He twisted in his seat to shake hands. "How d'you do," he nodded politely. "Alec."

"Hi. Man, you must have been worried sick about the crash. Chess barely slept that night. Do you think he's okay for today?"

It took Alec a moment to recover from being startled. Chess had been that worried about him?

"Racing is a family," Sally added, not impatient but immediately understanding. "I was surprised, too. It's great to meet you."

"We wondered about Ty for a while," Kiera added, propping her elbows on her knees as she grinned. "Figured he wasn't ready to settle down. I had no idea…"

"Oh, come on. We had *some* idea." Sally winked.

Alec nodded slightly, his cheeks burning. "Ah. Yeah. I mean, I'm pretty new to… dating him."

"Aw! You're jumping in the deep end, hon," Kiera laughed, then gestured. "Come on, sit with us."

Alec's nerves were no better, but he sure as hell appreciated the offer. It was nice not to sit alone, stewing in his worry over Tyler's safety.

When he took a seat next to them, Sally leaned over Kiera to get a look at him. "You look like you saw a ghost. Are you nervous for him?"

As soon as Alec nodded, she patted his knee. "You need something to eat. I'll grab a hot dog for you. Back in a minute."

Before he could open his mouth and say that he was all right, she was gone.

Kiera chuckled. "Don't stop her when she goes into Mom mode."

Alec rubbed his cheeks and nodded, unable to help a quiet laugh. "I appreciate it. Yeah. I've been a little… I mean, he kind of snuck back to it."

"No way." Kiera scoffed and shook her head. "I thought he'd learned last time."

"Last time?"

Kiera hesitated, then seemed to figure there was no harm in telling him. "He got into a wreck a couple years ago—right after he started driving this car, actually. Came back way too soon."

"And was he… okay?" Alec hadn't realized he was twisting apart the napkin that had been on his seat until just now. He brushed the pile of paper from his knee to the ground and shook his head.

"Yeah. Not exactly top-20 finish, but he did okay." Kiera patted his arm. "I know it's hard to take advice, but: relax.

This is his job. He knows what he's doing. That said, I wanna smack my husband sometimes for the stuff he does."

Alec laughed under his breath. "Yeah. You can say that again."

Sally came back, and Alec realized how hungry he was the moment he smelled the hot dog. He wolfed it down while they grinned.

"Yeah, it's easy to get caught up in their lives," Sally told him. "Was Kiera just giving you the talk?"

"More or less," Alec mumbled when he'd swallowed. "How do you do it? I mean—marrying him," he nodded at Kiera. "Not knowing if he'll come home."

"Fatalities are really, really rare these days," Sally told him, her voice soft.

Kiera nodded. "And safety standards... they're way higher. It pisses the guys off, but it's good, too. That crash he was in? Super rare."

"Then why did it happen?" Alec shook his head. "Ty told me he thinks it was deliberate."

"They check out all the video footage afterward. The investigators must have found... ohhh. But wait." Sally straightened up, then gripped Kiera's hand. "Remember the Deux hardware store sponsorship?"

"Yeah."

Alec was lost, but he nodded along.

"Well, they just put out their whole LGBT acceptance policy, like, last year, right?"

"Right," Alec murmured.

Sally looked like she was trying to explain, gesturing her hands a few times before she formed words. "Okay, so... they yanked sponsorship from Ty last season, and picked up one of Richie's teammates... Derek. Ty's current sponsor is this big auto parts store, Spare Tire... well, I don't know. I don't think they've said a lot about gay people."

Alec was catching up. "You think Richie and his team are targeting Ty? Is there a grudge?"

"No more than any rivals." Kiera shrugged. "Not enough to try to kill a guy over."

Alec nodded, a chill running down his spine. "Are they trying to... I don't know, out him? Kill him? What's the deal?"

Sally drummed her fingers on her knee. "What if they're homophobic dicks? Can we assume that? I never liked Richie when I met him, and I tend to hate self-absorbed, homophobic pricks."

Alec liked her already. He grinned. "Yeah. So it's a... hate... bump?"

"But the sponsorship. Richie's sponsor is in a three-year contract, if I remember right." Kiera was searching on her phone. "Yeah. Two more years."

"Check Richie's teammates."

"Harry," they both said at the same time.

Alec looked back and forth between them. God, he was out of his depth. He was going to need to do some serious homework. "Harry?"

"He finished well in the race where Ty crashed. The best of the four cars. And he's got nearly as many individual points as Richie. I can't find out much about his sponsorship contract, but I think he's done this year."

"If Ty crashed and got replaced, Spare Tire could find another team to support. And they paid well. That's why Ty has such a big name—or the other way around. Whatever," Kiera waved a hand. "It's a lot of money, and teams like drivers who can bring a lot of money and a big sponsor, that's the important part."

Alec's head hurt. "Individual points… so… they want to…?" He shrugged helplessly.

"I think they're trying to sideline him because they want his money. If he happens to be gay and they happen to hate him for it…" Sally shook her head. "You need to talk to him and see if he and Richie ever fought, or…" she trailed off, then cleared his throat.

"Or fucked," Alec finished, half-smiling. The idea of a lover's quarrel gone horribly wrong made sense, and Ty had sure as hell seemed to hate the guy. But he'd put that down to the crash. "I will. Do you think they'll try anything this race?"

"Richie can't, unless he wants investigators crawling up his ass for months." Sally shook her head. "Unless he's retiring, and these guys don't retire until they're chained down. He wants to… wait."

"Wants to what?" Alec curled his fingers into the napkin that had held his hot dog, resisting the urge to shred this one, too. "Wants to?"

Sally put a hand on his arm and drew a breath, and he mirrored her. When he was calmer, she continued, "Wants to move up to a team with even more prestige. Drivers switch teams—no pun intended—all the time."

Alec managed a weak chuckle. "So this sponsor would be better… but Harry's the one who'd get it?"

Kiera leaned in. "Good point. Okay. So, if they're working together—this could be the start of the plan, you know? Set themselves up with good sponsors, buy their way to better cars and teams and a name in lights. But not directly, or people would notice. If Richie took out Ty and then got his sponsorship, that would be too obvious."

"So, slowly, over a few seasons." Alec started to understand. "All four of the drivers?"

"I dunno. But it sure as hell looks like it."

"Richie, Harry, and—who are the others?"

She rattled off their car numbers, and Alec trie to memorize them. "So Richie's not looking to impress people. They want Harry to finish really well. Which explains why he's been finishing ahead of the rest of them all season."

"Were they getting Ty out of the way to make a better finish for Harry last race?"

"We'd have to see the replay to make sure," Kiera murmured, shaking her head. "But we can totally go to Roger about this. He can put a word in someone's ear to look at the whole team. It wasn't like Harry finished first last time or anything. That would have been way too obvious. Guys have tried that before."

Alec shook his head and combed a hand through his hair, trying to stay calm. Normally, it was easy. Right now, here in the stands with nothing he could do, no way. "Can we warn Ty?"

"No way. It's gonna start any time now," Kiera murmured, resting a hand on his arm to keep him in his seat. "He won't get messages until after the race. Trust him—and his spotter. Great guy. He'll keep Ty safe."

He didn't last time, Alec wanted to say, but he drew a breath and let it out.

They were right. The whole time, Tyler had been sure Richie was up to something. He was going to be damn well aware of him this race, and no doubt his other teammates.

From what he'd said, he hadn't been aiming to finish first, anyway. He wasn't a threat to Harry's finishing position.

Why the fuck did this have to be such a big deal? And what the hell had Tyler got himself wrapped up in?

I thought racing was just cars going around a track for ages.

As he grew aware of the nearly-full stands around them and the rumble of car engines, all Alec could do was take a deep breath.

"Here we go," Kiera murmured, leaning in. "Get ready for a long couple hours."

Fuck, Tyler better be okay, so Alec could kick his ass—and then hug him. There was nothing he could do to keep him away from those assholes, and God knew he'd tried.

All he could do was watch as stillness settled over the stands, everyone holding their breath and waiting for the starting flag.

Kiera was on the phone, murmuring into it, but Alec felt sick as he watched the cars shoot off the starting line.

As long as Tyler made it through this race, they could find out the truth behind their theory. The odds were stacked against him, but that never seemed to stop him.

Goddamn it. He was pissed off at Tyler, but a little proud, too.

He would be just as glad to have him in his arms, safe and sound and next to him on the couch again, though.

But if this was what Tyler wanted to do, Alec wasn't going to stand in his way. Alec would be by his side—at least, whenever he wasn't sweating it out alone in the car, turn by hundred-plus-mile-an-hour turn.

Somehow, I love every inch of his attitude and stubbornness and goddamn sweet heart. Just please, please, let him be okay so I get the chance to tell him as much.

Chatter started up around him as people who obviously

saw each other every week caught up with each other, but Alec was oblivious as the minutes slid by.

Sally and Kiera stayed mostly apart from the talk and drinks, explaining what had happened sometimes when the crowd gasped, cheered, or chanted a driver's name, when a car pulled off the track into the pits, or especially when they seemed to jostle for position.

It all happened so fast—almost terrifyingly so—in real life. Not watching it on a screen made all the difference, and suddenly, the adrenaline rush made complete sense to Alec.

It wasn't until someone tapped his shoulder that Alec was forced to tear his eyes from the track.

An older man stood there in a plain polo shirt, but it was obvious from the way Sally was looking at him that this was someone important.

"Roger Hanwell," the guy introduced himself.

Hanwell... isn't that the team name? Alec caught his breath and straightened up, offering his hand to shake. "Alec. Pleased to meet you."

"You, too, son. Kiera just told me what she thinks is going on. I've passed the word on. They're not gonna stop the race or anything, but there are folks looking at the crash investigation again. If anything weird happens again, and if they find anything, they could DQ the team."

Alec nodded slowly. "So someone's listening."

"Yeah. It's a serious accusation, but I'll put my name behind it." Roger squeezed Sally's shoulder. "These are smart cookies. And Ty himself told me he thinks there was something off about the crash. Besides, I think Josh would have throttled me otherwise."

Alec blinked as he looked beyond Roger and saw Josh edging his way down the row of seats.

Josh grinned and raised a hand in a wave. "Sorry I couldn't make it 'til now. Farm shit to sort out. Everything fine so far?" He looked down at the track, seemingly reading it the way everyone around Alec seemed to be able to do.

"So far, so good." Roger nodded between them. "I've gotta go, but I'll see you again afterward. Welcome to the family, kid." He offered his hand again.

Alec's heart soared.

Fuck, he hadn't realized how nervous he was—about meeting the team, about maybe accidentally outing Tyler to everyone around him, about making Tyler's work life worse. But these people had been nice to him so far, and so had Sarah.

Maybe, just maybe, this could work out.

CHAPTER

Twenty

TYLER

Everything hurt.

Every few seconds, when he moved his foot between the brake and gas, his ankle protested.

Keeping a firm, yet loose grip on the wheel made his wrist ache.

His forearm ached from holding his arms in nearly the same position for hours.

Hell, even his head was aching now that the temperature in the car was climbing. The fan blowing air up his back did little to counteract the sheen of sweat that had formed on his skin.

Keeping his breaths shallow so as not to aggravate his ribs made him feel like a dog in a locked car, but it was his own damn fault he'd gotten into this car.

And Tyler was so happy his cheeks hurt from smiling.

From the first purr of the engine, he'd felt like he was back at home. After weeks stuck out on the farm doing nothing, it was fucking heaven.

Fighting his pride had been hard. He'd wanted to fight for

a spot in the top 20, just like everyone else. But it hadn't taken him long to notice Richie deliberately hanging back.

His spotter had thought he was out of his mind when he told him he was going to stay behind Richie for the whole damn race. But, to his credit, he'd listened and directed Tyler accordingly.

"He's *waiting* to be overtaken again," his spotter spoke up, sounding bewildered. "He hates being ahead of you."

The hardest part had been finding his place behind Richie and following him to the pits and out again without being too obvious about it. The guys in the pit seemed to know the plan by now, and thankfully, they hadn't asked questions. Not that anyone had time for that.

Just in case he crashed out, he'd made sure to keep a car between himself and Richie. Last thing he needed was anyone thinking he was deliberately taking Richie out as revenge.

"Three to go," his spotter told him. Exactly what he wanted to hear. He could coast through a finish right in the middle of the pack.

It irritated him to let Richie take more points, but there was a damn good reason. If he had his way, Richie wasn't going to be keeping those for much longer.

The sweat running down the back of his neck made him shiver, giving him some welcome sensory distraction from the pain burning through him. He was dizzy and not sure his legs would support him afterward, but he could hold on for just three more laps.

Another minute, he promised himself. *Not long at all. Just focus.*

"He's making a move. Trying to get in the high line again."

Goddamn. It was hard to find an excuse and chance to

stay behind him, but Tyler poured his attention into it. It was the opposite of his usual skill—staying intentionally slow without endangering anyone was a lot harder than it looked.

Richie was in the high line and slowing. He saw a gap—not much of one, but enough.

Tyler didn't have a spare brain cell for another thought besides how to get in there now, and keep two cars between him and Richie. No way would Richie have time to make another move before the finish line.

He twitched the wheel, glided into the gap, and let out his breath slowly while his spotter gruffly barked in his ear that they were on the last lap.

"What am I at?"

"About forty."

Good enough. Not a great finish, but far from the worst. Looked like Richie would make thirty-seven or thirty-eight, something like that.

The next few minutes passed in a blur.

He barely remembered crossing the line, or slowing with everyone else, or shoving himself free of the car. Or the agony that ensued when his whole arm lit on fire.

He only had enough brain power to register the facts: his arm almost wouldn't move, and he couldn't get out of the car. He slumped, and there was a medical crew at his side almost right away.

Again. He was getting to make a habit of that.

It was gonna rain. Thank God the weather had held until now.

Tyler closed his eyes, and he grinned, and he curled the fingers of his good hand so tightly they protested, his nails digging into his palm.

He'd glimpsed Richie somewhere between the car and the stretched, and Richie looked pissed.

For today, by today's definition, he'd won.

"Hey, you."

Tyler's brain was sluggish. He recognized the feeling of an IV in the back of his hand, and the good drugs coursing through his body. His chest was tight, but he wasn't thirsty.

He did need to pee, though.

Fluids, too, then.

He managed to open his eyes. For a moment, he thought he was seeing double and blinked, but there were two guys in here with him.

Then his brain supplied names, and he smiled: Alec and Josh.

"Glad you guys are getting along," he mumbled.

Alec and Josh swapped looks, and he couldn't tell which of them made which snorting noise.

Tyler grinned woozily. "So that went okay. Right?" He was fairly sure it had. The fragments coming back to him told him as much.

"You let Richie beat you." Josh shook his head. "And good thing. Roger was just in."

"And?"

"Uh. There's mixed news."

Alec scoffed. "Your sponsor doesn't like that the TV cameras saw me."

"*I* like that you saw me." Tyler grinned, and he found he couldn't look away from Alec. God, he was pretty. It was surreal to see him in this setting, but then, it wasn't too far from how they'd first met. Alec looked sexy in a white coat.

"And," Alec added, "Roger pretty much told them to fuck off. It was kind of cool."

"Roger's cool." Tyler managed a slow thumbs-up, then tried wiggling all his fingers and toes. All working. Good."

"And they caught Richie's whole damn team cheating," Josh burst out with, unable to contain himself a moment longer.

Well, duh. That hadn't been an accidental threat before the last race he'd been in.

Tyler raised his brows slowly. He could hardly feel his face. These were the *really* good drugs. "How?"

"Bumper shape. Not conforming to… something about a new car shape," Alec shook his head. "Roger looked like he wanted to tear someone apart. Kiera and Sally figured it out. Something to do with them wanting your sponsorship. Apparently they've been talking to Harry already. It was all set up. He confessed, like, instantly. Richie wouldn't admit to anything. Cops are involved. The whole nine yards."

"You know, Alec nearly pulled the doctor card to get in here and see you," Josh added, grinning. "Roger pretty much told them all they could go to hell."

Yeah. Roger was good like that. "I wouldn't suck his dick, but he's cool," Tyler murmured.

Alec burst out laughing, and then Tyler became aware of Alec's hand in his. "I'm glad," Alec told him.

Tyler tried to tilt his head on the pillow. "That mean you're not dumping me?"

"I've got some yelling to do first," Alec told him.

"I'm going away now," Josh muttered in the background.

"So you can be all gross and coupley." He breezed out quickly.

"Thanks." Tyler glanced back at Alec. "Can we save the yelling? The curtains are pretty thin here."

Alec scoffed and shook his head, then squeezed his hand. "Of course. There's more available on request."

"Good." Tyler couldn't come up with a snappy comeback, so he just gazed at Alec for long enough that Alec turned red.

"What?"

"I love you."

Alec opened his mouth, then closed it again and chuckled. "You're high on painkillers." He looked embarrassed.

Tyler didn't understand why Alec was fidgeting, and he pressed, "But I do. Is it something I did?"

Alec flicked his finger against the back of Tyler's hand gently. "Yeah. Sneaking off to race against some psycho killer asshole when I love your dumb ass and I just wanted you to be… be safe." Alec's eyes glistened.

"That's the most romantic thing anyone's ever said. When I quote it to my brothers, can I include the crying?"

Alec's laugh was rich. He wiped his eyes and let go of Tyler's hand, flopping into the chair by the bed. "You are *such* an asshole."

"Apparently you love assholes," Tyler said. His laugh was more of a giggle. "Pun not intended but totally awesome. Get it? Because you…"

That set Alec off into a flood of laughter of his own. "I get it. Shut up, before they throw me out."

"Just tell 'em you're my doctor," Tyler grinned broadly at Alec.

Alec groaned. "Don't. Roger figured it out when he called

Doc Gordon. He gave me a hell of a side-eye before we got in here."

"He won't get us in trouble," Tyler stated confidently. He knew Roger well enough to be sure of that.

"We both narrowly escaped trouble," Alec said, his voice quieter. "Can we just… take it easier now?"

Tyler nodded slightly. "Except I'll be racing for real next time," he told Alec. "Can you handle that?"

"If you don't keep secrets from me again. If you're gonna do something stupid, don't you ever sneak off again."

Tyler drew a breath and let it out. He had plenty of people who cared, but it meant something different coming from Alec. Especially since Alec loved him. "Yeah. I won't."

"Good. Even if you're drugged-up, I'm gonna hold you to that," Alec told him firmly.

Tyler snorted. "That doesn't sound strictly…" He squinted, trying to find words. "Legal?"

"I'll give *you* illegal," Alec muttered, shaking his head. "Worrying the crap out of me. And Josh. Vanishing. Fainting when you got out of the car. Jesus Christ."

Tyler fumbled until he gripped Alec's hand again. "Thank you."

Despite his disgruntled words, Alec's gaze was soft as he gazed at Tyler. "You're welcome."

With Alec's hand in his, Tyler felt like everything was gonna work out just fine.

Twenty~One

TYLER

"Oh, look who's here!"

For the first time in his life, Tyler couldn't quite make eye contact with his brothers—or even Alec. He waved, glancing around at the sea of familiar faces before jerking his chin toward the bar. "I'm getting drinks. Anyone?"

A couple of them needed refills, so he counted them up on his fingers and then nodded. "Back in a minute."

Alec stayed at the table with them, which Tyler was glad to see. At least he felt comfortable enough with them now to do that.

"Hey, Tom. Four beers, please," Tyler greeted the bartender, but his mind was elsewhere.

"The whole gang's here again? I think you guys need a loyalty card," Tom joked as he pried caps off bottles.

"Hell, we need to buy a table," Tyler chuckled.

Tom pushed the bottles over the counter and took his bills, opening the register. He glanced over it for a moment as if unsure, catching Tyler's attention. Then, he plunged ahead. "I saw your interview. Before that race."

"Oh." Tyler wasn't used to being recognized while he was out with his friends. Normally people here were good about pretending they were all just nobodies. He fumbled to adopt his professional attitude. "Uh, thanks. It was a pleasure to get back to racing."

"That race beat the crap out of you. Did they really wheel you off? Major respect, man."

Tyler internally winced. Exactly what he didn't want to think about—and what he owed a few people apologies for. Still, he managed to keep his expression neutral. "Thanks," he said lightly. "Yeah, they did."

"You good for next week? We've been thinking about getting a TV so we can support our hometown boy."

Tyler cleared his throat. "Yeah, I'm racing next week. It won't be pretty, but I'm not missing another race, God help me."

He didn't want to say that they'd chosen this bar originally because it was a bit of a dive. It wasn't a sports bar, and it wasn't a preppy place with music video screens everywhere. No fancy shit, just solid tables and booths, cheap beer, and good service.

"Here ya go." Tom handed back his change.

"Thanks." Tyler left a few bills on the counter, saluting with one bottle as he picked them up between his fingers. He tried not to hurry back to the table—not that he could walk fast. Despite himself, he had to limp to keep his leg from going out from under him.

Once again, all eyes turned to him, and Alec half-rose as if to help before settling back down.

Tyler slid one across the table to Alec and the other two to Roman and Nico.

It was surprising that all of them had made it tonight:

Oscar had managed to wiggle out of some kind of choreography rehearsal, and Leo had finished up a photo shoot early. Tyler felt even shittier because of it.

"Look who's all fancy."

Tyler tugged at his tie, loosening it. "Gotta dress up to go to the opera."

"Oh, that was tonight!" Deen grinned and looked over at Alec. "Did our learned friend enjoy himself?"

"Hard to tell," Alec admitted, grinning. "He kept giving me confused looks, but he didn't applaud in the middle of an act like a rookie."

Tyler laughed. "I've been to Oscar's shows. I know my shit now. No applauding just 'cause everyone else is doing it, no heckling…"

In truth, he'd felt completely out of place among the older crowd. It seemed like everyone around him understood Italian, or did a good job pretending. He could kind of get the gist of the action from body language, but there was a lot of stopping and singing that just confused him. At least musicals were in English.

"I think it's sweet he went anyway," Roman grinned wickedly. "Our little lovebird."

Tyler flipped off Roman, but he put his arm around Alec's shoulder. He could feel Alec beaming without even looking at him. The sheer unadulterated joy was unmistakable, and so sweet he couldn't resist sneaking a glance.

Crap. Now he was blushing.

"Oh, that's a nice color," Josh grinned and elbowed him. Tyler smacked him back, and Josh reached out to tussle before pulling back. "Ah, yeah. I'll go easy on you."

"Fuck off," Tyler grumbled.

That brought the conversation back to his injuries—all of which had worsened again, Doc Gordon had confirmed.

"It's your own damn fault," Blane added, eyeing him. "He was at least walking last week, wasn't he?"

His brothers nodded, and Tyler sighed. No sense beating around the bush. "So, uh… sorry I was a dumbass." He raised his beer slightly toward Josh and Alec in particular. "I kinda snuck off."

Josh eyed him. "Yeah, I thought you were up to something. Wasn't until Alec showed up asking where you'd been all week that I put two and two together."

"Yeah." Tyler grimaced. "I was going out of my mind not doing anything… you know that."

"You can't sit still for three minutes anyway," Nico said with a laugh. "I'm just surprised it wasn't sooner."

"Yeah," Tyler nodded, then cleared his throat and straightened up. "But it was a big risk. I only realized that… well, after the race. It took everything I had."

"But you're still going back," Deen murmured. "When you find your passion, it's like that."

Nico glanced at Deen, then back at Tyler. He sighed. "I just wish his weren't so…"

"Risky?" Tyler suggested. "Yeah. More so when there's a maniac on the loose."

Alec nudged him. "Have you heard more?"

"The whole team's been disqualified. They might get pulled from the whole season—investigators are working on it now. It's a big scandal. And weirdly, it seems to have overshadowed… my whole big coming out thing."

"Which isn't that big, it turns out," Dustin said. "I was looking up the threads the other day."

"How do you find these threads? Do you just Google me?" Tyler squinted. "Actually, never mind. I don't want to know." He heard enough in the whispers and side-glances in real life. He didn't need people's thoughts, too. "I just thought I should say sorry. It's my own neck on the line, but… you guys worry, too. That can't be easy."

Alec squeezed his thigh tightly and leaned into him. Tyler could tell Alec was proud of him for saying the words.

"You're happy, though," Josh spoke up, glancing at the others as they nodded. "It's great to see you less touchy about everything. That might be from getting laid, though."

Tyler laughed. "Probably. But yeah, I was kind of a jerk."

"Don't do it again," Josh said with a shrug. "And if you're gonna do something stupid, at least let me drive you there so you can save your energy. Christ."

Tyler saw Alec glance at him meaningfully, and his cheeks burned. "Yeah. Uh. If I do stupid shit, I'll tell you guys about it." Honestly, if he had to tell people he was doing something dumb *before* he did it, it might stop him from doing it so much.

Which was good all around, really.

The silence that settled was much less awkward, but Tyler's chest felt tight.

He had a bunch of guys—even a boyfriend—who weren't demanding he stop doing what made him feel most alive. They just wanted to be there and support him when he did.

How fucking lucky was he?"

"So, wedding planning," Deen announced, while Nico looked sheepish but pleased with himself.

"No shit," Tyler exclaimed. "I thought you guys were just gonna be engaged for a while."

"I thought about it," Deen said, then grinned and looked at Nico. "I mean, we thought about it."

Nico snorted. "No, he means *he* thought about it and told me the wedding's this year." He gave Deen a good-natured grin.

Tyler knew Nico. He was a lot more sentimental than he let on. If Deen wanted something, Nico would do his damnedest to make sure he got it.

Not unlike himself and Alec. They might be new, but Tyler saw a road ahead, and a reason to make it work. He was ready to do what it took to see that kind of smile on Alec's face.

It was clear as daylight. Fuck. Drugged-up words aside, *this* was love.

He didn't have a clue how they'd make it work yet, but just getting to tuck Alec against his side out here in public? Worth all their back-and-forth and uncertainty, and the tough conversations coming up.

Knowing that Alec was here for him every bit as much as his brothers, but with that quiet, cool confidence of a man who was certain in his desire for Tyler...

It was hot and incredible and made him feel like he'd won the lottery. He didn't have words. He just had a visual—the two of them on a road trip through life. A full tank of gas, hand in hand, an open road ahead.

There was no need to put the pedal to the metal now. They had all the time and space in the world.

Tyler nodded along with everyone else as Deen explained the wedding. Alec was listening—he'd ask him for the details later. For now, he had some very important daydreaming.

"I don't even like this place anymore," Tyler admitted, laughing. He was a little drunk, and that helped soothe the ache.

Alec steered him in, finding the living room and making sure he plopped on the couch. "And no wonder. At the top of those fucking stairs."

"Falcon once—he once lived in a *top* floor place. Like, two or three flights of stairs. So that's why his best friend, Oscar… you know, the dancer?"

"I know who Oscar is," Alec assured him, looking like he was trying not to laugh.

"Falcon was staying with—I mean, Oscar was staying with Falcon. On the top floor. Which was why he had to stay with Roman when he got hurt and quit dancing. And that's how they met. Whew, my tolerance has gone down," Tyler lamented. "Not enough parties."

Alec came back into the room, carrying a couple glasses of water. "Aspirin?"

"Bathroom cabinet."

When Alec handed over the pills, Tyler swallowed them and grinned at him. "Thanks, baby."

Alec made a *tsch* noise and wrapped his arm around Tyler's shoulders. "You have to be on the road again tomorrow, don't you? You don't want a hangover. Drink up."

Tyler just gazed at Alec for a few moments. He'd missed the important part of that story. "So I think you know how they all met now. And when they did, one by one… it felt like…"

Alec was quiet now, gazing at him.

Tyler swallowed hard and plunged ahead. "I thought I couldn't find someone that fit me. They're all great guys.

They—shh," he patted Alec's hand when Alec tried to interrupt, no doubt to bolster his confidence. "I know I'm awesome. But they have… they have stable lives."

"And I already told you I don't care," Alec murmured, rubbing his shoulder gently. Then, he grinned. "I like that you know you're awesome."

Tyler grinned back. "Sure I am. But being cool to hang out with isn't like… being… someone you could marry."

Oh, crap. He hadn't meant to go *there* quite so soon. He knew he was blushing. Hopefully the alcohol flush that had come over him would hide it.

Alec chuckled, slipping his hand into Tyler's. "I dunno. I think we should live together first. Meet your family."

"Not yours?"

Alec hesitated, then shook his head. "I'll tell you later. What I mean is, you're only back in town for like, a day every week at best, right?"

"Yeah, pretty much. Until the season's over in November. I get January and February off."

Alec nodded. "So, move in with me."

Tyler blinked a few times, then stared at Alec, trying to read him. Alec wasn't joking, though. "Really? I mean, my lease is up in August. That's only a couple months away."

"Good. Let's plunge in."

Tyler beamed so widely his cheeks hurt. "Alec Lands. I do believe I've been making you a *little* more reckless." Alec's blush was totally worth it. Tyler cackled and added, "Next thing I know, you'll be doing handbrake turns in the Walmart parking lot."

"Oh, shut up," Alec laughed. "It's a good thing you're…" He trailed off.

Tyler hesitated, almost afraid to breathe. He wasn't sure what Alec was about to say.

Hot? Yeah, he'd picked up plenty of guys who thought he was. *Rich?* Same deal. *Smart?* Alec seemed to think so, even if Tyler disagreed.

Alec smiled gently at him and squeezed his hand. "You."

It took a few seconds for that to sink in. Then, Tyler closed his eyes and pulled Alec into him for the tightest hug his fucked-up arm could manage.

"I meant it when I said I love you. I thought racing was everything to me, but… I'm ready to learn about the power of love."

Alec snorted. "Really? Air Supply?"

Tyler grinned. "Come on. You're my baby, and I'm your man."

"Oh, stop deflecting," Alec sighed, rubbing his back. "I love you for you. Death-defying stunts included. You're trouble for me, but I wouldn't have it any other way."

"Britney? Now who's deflecting?" Tyler laughed and rested his head on Alec's shoulder. Just for a few moments, while he thought about all the things he wanted to do with Alec.

It was almost enough to make him want to take all the time off he could. Hell, he could skip the afterparties and get a little more time with this man…

"C'mon," Alec murmured after silence had fallen for a minute. "You're dozing off."

"Doc Gordon would prefer I did that in bed," Tyler mumbled. His joints were stiff. Had he actually been napping?

Alec chuckled, pulling him to his feet slowly, a hand on his hip. "And so would I."

Tyler was too sleepy to manage a smartass response, so he just smiled and followed Alec to his bed.

He couldn't wait to get rid of his bed and move into *their* bed. Together, for whatever precious time they could carve out of their lives.

Yeah. This felt right.

Twenty~Two

ALEC

For the first time, Alec resented the sunlight pouring through the slats of the window blinds.

It meant Tyler was about to leave, and they'd wasted precious hours together in sleep. On the other hand, it was the best sleep he could remember in years.

With Tyler carefully tucked in his arms, half-curled in the only sleeping position he could manage without pain, Alec had felt like even Tyler's bare apartment was home.

The morning sunlight warmed the cool white paint, making this bedroom feel like their own cozy nest. A retreat from the rest of the world, for just a few hours.

Still, he preferred his own room.

"Mmngh," Tyler murmured, slowly stretching.

Alec caught his breath. Had he been fidgeting too much? He'd tried to stay still, however hard it was to resist playing with Tyler's hair or tracing a finger along his bare back.

God, he was gorgeous, even scruffy and sleepy.

"Morning?" Tyler mumbled. "What is this shit? Light?"

Alec grinned. "I know. I was just thinking that." He didn't have to add, *Because you're leaving sooner.*

Tyler shifted and rolled over to face him, slipping his hand into Alec's. "You sleep okay?"

Alec nodded and kissed Tyler, then ran his other hand down his shoulder and side. "Perfectly. Got a hangover?"

"Nope. I don't get 'em much anyway," Tyler said with a cheeky grin. "Lucky me."

"Lucky you," Alec echoed. "But you'll be staying away this week, right? So you can heal better?"

"Yes, sir," Tyler said, the pillow rustling when he nodded against it.

They both jolted when Alec's phone went off.

This early? Who the hell is that?

"Sorry," Alec mumbled, rolling away to grab his phone off the bedside table. Unfamiliar with the layout, he nearly knocked the lamp off but grabbed it in time. His heart was still racing as he answered, "Hey."

"Alec?"

There was only one person that could be.

"Hey, Mom." He pushed himself to sit upright, his heart already pounding. God, his palms were getting all sweaty again.

Next to him, Tyler sat up, but his focus had narrowed to the voice on the other end of the line.

For years, he'd daydreamed about getting this call. His parents would tell him they'd come around. Maybe they'd seen a friendly gay on TV, or someone they knew had talked sense into them, or the reverend had guilted them into loving their own kid. Whatever the reason, they'd apologize for being such dicks.

Sometimes, when he had this fantasy, it was a loving

reunion as he started sobbing on the phone. *Yes, I missed you. For so many damn years.* Other times, he rejected them. *Fuck off. You weren't there for me when I needed it; you don't get to claim credit for me turning out all right.*

He couldn't think what to say now.

"Sally told me that Barbara said…" He tuned out the rest of the irrelevant information, and a bittersweet smile touched his lips. His mom had always done this—rambled through all the details before getting to the point of the story. "—that she saw you in the parking lot at church a few weeks ago."

Crap. Of course someone had seen him.

He'd almost forgotten that day and the glimpse at the past he'd worked so hard to leave behind.

"Yeah. I was deciding whether this new reverend's a good guy or an asshole like the last one."

"Language, Alec!"

Ah, it was just like old times. Missing the forest for the trees—the meaning was less important than the words he used in making his point. Or, rather, she used the words as a convenient excuse to ignore the meaning.

"I was deciding whether this reverend was a real Christian, or he's just in it for the chance to repress his own homosexual desires."

"Alec Lands, I never want to hear you suggest such a thing again. You haven't changed a bit."

"News flash, Mom. Neither have you. People don't change. Once a gay, always a gay. Once a self-serving jerk looking for an excuse to feel like a victim, always a parent who should be ashamed of themselves."

A hand rested on his arm, and he cast Tyler a distracted smile. He wasn't upset—he didn't even sound it.

"The nerve. The sheer nerve of you, trying to upset your own parents."

"You stopped being my parents when you threw me out," Alec said dryly. "I don't owe you respect when you won't give me any. What do you want? A band-aid for your guilt?"

"I want you to give up… these… TV appearances."

It took Alec a few seconds to even figure out what that meant. Then, he started to laugh. "Give up these… you mean… Dad was watching the race?"

"The TV camera *showed* you in the stands. They're saying you're some driving man's boyfriend."

"Too bad, Mom. Guess you'll have to explain how love works to your church group. It would sure help if you felt any yourself. Bye." Alec hung up and tossed his phone aside, taking a deep breath as Tyler pulled him in for a long, tight hug.

He braced himself for the questions, but they didn't come. Tyler said nothing.

Alec appreciated it more than he could find words to express. He buried his face in Tyler's shoulder and wrapped his arms around him. He'd thought he was relaxed until the moment the stress he hadn't even realized he was holding melted away.

Fuck. I need him.

"Are you gonna be okay today?" Tyler sounded worried. "I can try to rearrange things—"

"No," Alec murmured. "I'm fine. Unless I can persuade you to rest more."

"Aren't we a couple stubborn assholes?" Tyler laughed quietly, rubbing Alec's shoulder.

Alec nodded slightly, pulling back enough to rest his head on Tyler's shoulder, his legs curled under him as he found a comfortable spot. "Well, now you know the deal with my family."

"I had a feeling something was going on," Tyler frowned. "I'm sorry. How long has it been?"

"Oh, God. Years and years. But I've spent so long wondering whether I'm good enough to be their son… I'm over that now. But I wonder sometimes if it changed the whole way I think."

Tyler sighed and nodded. "Brains are funny that way." He pulled back to make Alec look at him, those eyes for once serious and fixed on him. "I'm not really a words guy, but… I need you to know that you're enough for *me*."

"Even if I don't race, and party, and… stuff?" Alec murmured. He was almost afraid to look at him, but Tyler wasn't letting him squirm away.

"I don't want that. It's the lifestyle that comes with the stuff I like doing, but it doesn't mean I find it attractive," Tyler said.

That made so much sense that the clarity was almost blinding. "Oh," Alec whispered.

"And whatever's ordinary and grounded and routine about your life? I like that," Tyler added firmly. "Mine is pretty crazy. Being with you makes me remember to slow down."

Alec's chest felt so warm he could barely breathe. "Really?" He knew he was glowing.

"Really," Tyler said, mirroring his smile. "I'll introduce you to my family. They'll love you. And you've got a crazy bunch of brothers now."

"I do?"

"You do." Tyler nudged him. "They're always going out for lunches and drinks and stuff. There's so many of us now that someone's always online to text, too. I'll make sure you get added so you can meet up with everyone while I'm away."

Alec managed a shaky laugh. It was almost too good to be true. "And you… you're okay with not seeing me much?"

"If you are," Tyler said. "I'm happy like this. We can try an open relationship if you want. Whatever you want."

He really means it. Whatever I want. Oh, man. Alec beamed. "I'm happy, too. If the dry spells get too long, I'll travel and see you some weekends when you're racing at nearby tracks."

Tyler chuckled and rubbed Alec's shoulder. "Oh, that would be a great way to celebrate the ass I'm gonna kick as I get back into it."

He really was incorrigible. Alec grinned and shook his head. "And you know, if we spend too long apart, I might just be demanding when we see each other again."

Tyler lit up. "I am a hundred percent fine with this."

"Good," Alec laughed and pulled Tyler against him gently, resting a hand on his chest. "I gotta start getting ready for work."

"Me too."

Already, Alec felt the anticipation of their next day together thrumming through them. Next time, with no opera and no brothers and no real life to intrude, they could make the most of it.

He couldn't wait for Tyler to be healed up, so that strong, flexible body could be put to good use.

"I hope you're not thinking of work." Tyler poked the sheets between his legs, where they tented.

Alec laughed and slapped Tyler's hand away. "I'm thinking of a former patient, actually. I hope he's back to himself very, very soon."

"Think we've got time for you to explain these thoughts?" Tyler smirked. "It looks like the kind of stuff I'd be into."

"Oh, yeah." Alec shifted until he straddled Tyler, grinning down at him. "I'll explain it. I've got a gifted tongue."

Tyler groaned and wrapped his hands around Alec's shoulders as Alec started to kiss his way down his chest. "God, I love you. Dating you was the best idea ever."

Alec laughed. "It was, and I love you too, baby. Now shut up and let me suck you off."

Tyler winked. "Yes, sir!"

Alec had found his rock, and he came with a rock of his own. God, he'd gotten luckier than he'd ever imagined.

No more *this is enough for now*, and no more *I shouldn't have*. It just worked between them—as easy as that.

Twenty~Three

TYLER, TWO MONTHS LATER

"HOW GAY DO YOU THINK MOTORSPORTS ARE?"

Tyler had been prepared to answer *what's it like being the first gay driver*, not this question. He stopped, then laughed.

His interviewer, Mac, mirrored the grin and waited, pencil poised on paper. The recorder between them on the hotel room desk was running, too.

He'd done a hell of a lot of interviews over the last couple months, and most of them had focused on *the gay thing* for a question or two before hurriedly switching focus to something else.

This was a gay magazine, though. Tyler had had no idea what to expect, but he was already glad he'd said yes. They'd warned him that if this went well, he could expect more. At this rate, he'd need a publicist of his own.

Fine by him.

"Uh, it depends how you mean," Tyler answered, trying to figure out how he wanted to put it. "There are a lot more gay people in the racing world than are willing—or able—to admit it. Like it's something that *needs* to be admitted. It should just be a fact. We ain't there yet, though."

Boy, had he learned that over the last few months.

Reactions had been mixed, but overall, more positive than he'd feared. Most of the guys closest to him—pretty much everyone on his team, in either the *playing for* or *working for* senses—had already known.

"You're saying there are more drivers who haven't come out yet?" Mac watched him intently.

Tyler hesitated. He wasn't going to name anyone, but even saying there were could start people searching for them.

"I'd guess so. We're a few percent of the population—there's bound to be a few more out there. Drivers, mechanics, owners, who knows? I've been lucky my team supported me through all this. That comes down to the team culture, and Roger's responsible for that. There's other teams out there who would never hire me now."

"Right," Mac said. He made a note. "Speaking of support, your sponsor—Spare Tire—has just put out a diversity policy for employees. Is that your doing?"

Tyler laughed. "I wouldn't know how to start with that. I had a hand in it, sure, but a lot smarter people figured out how to make it work."

"But you were involved in creating it? And you decided to do that, even when Deux offered you a lot of money to bail and be their face again? Is that related?"

"Sort of. Spare Tire got in touch long before Deux, er, dropped Richie. They said they didn't know what they were doing, but they wanted to be the kind of store where everyone felt welcome. Like my team has welcomed me with open arms. We're out there—up to ten percent of the population, some people think. And I have a lot of female fans who know their car shit—sorry," Tyler added, glancing at the recorder guiltily. "Can I swear?"

"Go for it," Mac laughed.

"They know their shit, but they get treated like *oh, silly dears trying to buy a spark plug*. And even the ones who don't know what they're doing wanna be treated like any old guy walking in, you know? Spare Tire was aware of this—we all know, don't we? But they didn't know how to challenge it. They're starting with a hiring diversity policy and they're encouraging their store managers to take training on how to be more inclusive."

"That's a lot of activism that will make a big difference, for a guy who says he's not very smart," Mac pointed out, grinning.

Tyler scoffed. "That's what my boyfriend's always saying. I always say I just drive cars. For some reason, people pay me to look silly in my skintight outfit and say nice things. I've often felt invisible. I never really worried I'd get kicked off the team spectacularly, but people's careers tend to slowly die if they break the mold."

"Right. And yours has done far from that."

Tyler took the compliment and nodded, grinning. "All because I feel comfortable being... totally me, now. If I can take the good experiences I've had and help other people feel that, too? Well, that's worth it all."

"Speaking of your boyfriend." Mac leaned in, and it was clear from his expression that he was dying of curiosity. "The gays have been abuzz."

Tyler laughed. "What do you want to know?"

"We've seen him supporting you at several races this

season. Rumor has it he works as a physical therapist. Is that how you met?"

"Maybe," Tyler answered with a coy smile. "We all like a sexy guy in a white coat, don't we?"

Mac laughed. "How does that work for you?"

"Oh, it's hard sometimes to be apart. But he gets weekends off, and I spend the odd weekday at home with him. We moved in last month, but I'm always joking I might as well be living on Mars."

"That sounds rough."

"But it's worth it," Tyler said without a shadow of a doubt. "My brothers—all my best friends—they've got my back. And Alec's at my side. It's a long road to recovery, and I wouldn't have made it without them."

"Are these guys the ones from high school?"

Mac had been doing his homework. Tyler was impressed. He raised an eyebrow and grinned. "Yeah, they are. Plus their boyfriends."

That made Mac nearly fall over. "Their boyfriends? So your friends have known for a while."

"Oh, God, yeah. It's been an open secret for years. Nobody wanted to know until now. I still don't know why they wanna know," Tyler laughed. "But if someone sees me and realizes they can race fast cars *and* fall for a guy, or fuck guys, or both? Maybe someone feels less alone? That's good. Being alone is hell, whether you're gay or straight or neither. Friends and family and significant broth—significant others," he caught himself just in time. "That's what makes life worth it."

"Before we go, I heard something else today. Apparently, Richie's been spotted down in New Orleans, holding the hand of another guy."

Tyler blinked a few times. He didn't hear that name much anymore. Not since the investigation had wrapped up and confirmed that it had been a coordinated, deliberate attempt at sabotage from all four drivers.

They'd all lost their sponsors and points, and the team was banned for the season.

It was cold comfort when Tyler still struggled with rib twinges through his pushups. He'd been doing well at building up the muscle that seemed to have evaporated during the endless recovery.

"Huh. Who knew?"

"Was there anything—you know, between you guys?" Mac raised an eyebrow, waiting expectantly.

Tyler laughed. "Come on. Just because a guy was rumored to be holding hands with another guy, you're gonna say he's gay? Twenty-first century. Even if he is, that'd be pretty fucked up. Lover's quarrel gone wrong? Nah. It all comes down to money."

It was up to Richie whether or not he decided to out himself.

After the interviewer left, Tyler stayed at the desk, weighing his phone up in his hand.

Fuck it, he finally decided. He could dig up that number with a few texts and not many questions asked.

It was the strangest text he'd ever composed, but pressing Send made his heart lighten.

A reporter cornered me today. Rumors of PDA with you & a guy. Told them it wasn't a lovers quarrel btwn us but gossip blogs never care about the truth. I don't either, so don't bother answering. If you try to tell them we ever dated or fucked I'll find a NOLA leather daddy to rip your balls off. I have better taste than you. Stay safe.

He sent Richie the text and shook his head. No matter what he'd done, nobody deserved to get dragged through the press without at least a heads-up.

What a weird damn life he had.

His phone went off a minute later.

Shame. The hate sex would have been great. Glad you're happy now. Stay safe too.

That was the closest to a *thank you* he was likely to get, but it was the most contact they'd had since the investigation wrapped up and the media firestorm subsided. Besides, it wasn't like he was ever gonna forgive Richie for what he'd done.

Sure, Richie was a young, idiot kid who had gotten caught up in the idea of buying his way to fame, but at the end of the day, he'd known the bumper was shaved. Anyone who knew anything knew how that could have ended.

Tyler shivered and pushed himself to his feet. Any time now, he had to leave for the meet-and-greet.

There was a knock on the door, and Tyler lit up. Only one person that could be. He opened the door and grabbed Alec in a hug. "Finally!"

"Yeah," Alec breathed into his shoulder, squirming closer to him. "Do I look ready to meet them? I don't feel ready."

"You look perfect," Tyler murmured. God, he'd missed this man. For good measure, he scooped Alec into his arms, beaming at the shocked expression on his face. "Missed you."

When Alec could speak again, he gasped, "Oh, my God. You *are* healed!" He fanned himself with one hand and looped his arm around Tyler's neck. "Got enough time to fuck me before we leave?"

It had been a long fucking ten days and two races since their last rendezvous, but there was no way they could risk it. Tyler laughed and cradled Alec against his chest, kissing him until he couldn't breathe. "'Fraid not."

"Damn," Alec breathed. "But you can do that again to tide me over. And the sex better be coming soon."

"Coming as soon as we can, baby."

Tyler kissed Alec as slowly and gently and passionately as he deserved for being by his side, both near and from afar, through these long weeks.

The only thing better than those weeks was bound to be the weeks—months—years ahead.

CHAPTER
Twenty-Four
ALEC

"They loved you, baby. Not as much as me, but almost. I'm the only one who gets to fuck that cute little ass." Tyler kicked the hotel room door shut and swept Alec up in a hug, slipping his fingers under the waistband of Alec's pants to cup his ass.

Alec burst out laughing. "And they say romance is dead."

"Romance is what we'll do as soon as I get you naked," Tyler promised, kissing Alec. "This is the consequence of telling me, *right before* four hours of shaking hands and signing photos, that you wanna fuck me."

Alec was guilty as charged, but he shot Tyler an innocent expression. "Me? That doesn't sound like me at all."

"I think you sprang a boner the moment I picked you up," Tyler said slowly, a wicked glint in his eye.

Alec tried to squirm out of Tyler's arms and make him work for it, but Tyler was already ripping their clothes off. Fuck, that desperation was hot.

They were naked within seconds, kicking their clothes aside as they ground against each other.

"You're gonna fuck me against the wall tonight," Alec told Tyler. He grinned and waited to see how his boyfriend took the command. Usually, it was *very well*.

Sure enough, Tyler growled and scooped him up, backing him up against the wall with a *thud* that sounded a lot worse than it felt.

"Yes," Alec panted in approval, and to show Tyler that he was fine. He didn't want to break the spell.

"You gonna stay still enough? If I drop you, you'll never let me forget it."

Alec laughed. "Guess we'll find out." He hoisted a leg around his lover's waist, then purred into his ear, "If you finish top twenty tomorrow, I'll even bend *you* over."

"If I win, will you handcuff me while you do it?" Tyler kissed Alec's neck in a tortuously slow pattern up to his earlobe.

Alec giggled. "Top five."

Tyler pulled back, looking startled. "Jesus. What do I get if I *win*?"

"You'll find out," Alec beamed.

Tyler growled and pressed him against the wall hard enough to grind their cocks together between their stomachs. "Tease."

"I'm not teasing. Just setting the stakes."

"If I lose?"

Alec considered this, hooking his ankle over his other leg to lock his legs around Tyler's waist. He judged Tyler's strength would be just fine for the job. "I might fuck you anyway," he told Tyler. "It's up to me, isn't it?"

Some days, he let Tyler ravish him, but Tyler was eager to please, and Alec loved seeing Tyler totally relaxed and confident.

Plus, riding him until he begged to be allowed to come was kind of the hottest thing ever.

"You're bossy as hell," Tyler told him before kissing him so hard he almost forgot he had a sassy retort to conjure up.

All Alec could manage when Tyler pulled away, leaving them both panting, was, "You love that."

"Yeah, I do." Tyler slid his cock between Alec's cheeks, teasing his hole.

God, that thick warmth and pressure felt divine. Alec rolled his head back against the wall and moaned. "Come on, baby."

For all his teasing, Alec needed him inside. Now.

"My lube's packed."

Alec made a *tsch* sound. "Should've been ready."

"I had an interview!" Tyler protested.

"That's no excuse," Alec grinned. "Check my jacket."

Tyler's grip faltered, sending an adrenaline rush clean through Alec's body. He tightened his grip a moment later, but Alec's heart pounded. "You brought *lube* to the first event I took you to?"

"Told you I wanted to fuck you soon," Alec informed him, grinning. "I half-considered asking the taxi driver to find a quiet street and take a walk."

In fact, he'd just wanted to make damn sure they'd get their chance tonight. He hadn't had two wet dreams in ten days in order to endure another two days.

God, Tyler made him horny on sight. Four hours being at his side, meeting fans who seemed to know more about cars than Alec would learn in the next twenty years, had been hell.

Four hours wanting to tear his tear clothes off and find the nearest bathroom stall.

But it was worth it. The anticipation made it even better. Even without Tyler inside him yet, his skin burned from head to toe, at every spot where their bodies touched.

"Our clothes are over there."

"How are your deadlifts?" Alec deadpanned, then unhooked his legs to gracefully drop to the ground. "Allow me."

He really should have expected it.

He bent over to grab the lube, and the moment it was in his hands, Tyler's arm went around his waist. He snagged the bottle clean out of Alec's hand.

Alec gasped as Tyler pushed him over the desk, two slick fingers pressing into him. "Someone's frisky!" That was about all he was gonna manage to say. God, his nerves lit up with pleasure at the thick, firm fingers that opened him up.

He fucking loved that, as much as Tyler might take orders, he also found every opportunity to disobey them. For all his quiet endurance, Alec knew he was a headstrong little thing, and Tyler was the first man to match him.

In all areas of life, not just the bedroom.

When Alec had suggested Tyler hold off racing, Tyler had listened to him, but he'd made up his own mind. When Tyler had suggested Alec punch homophobic athletes who suddenly didn't want him treating them after he came out, he had listened, but he'd decided he liked his medical license.

Slowly, more *family* had shown up. Guys who had never known whether to ask for a female physical therapist and risk being seen as pervs, or take a male physical therapist and risk the humiliation of explaining why they were popping a boner when physical instinct took over.

Wherever he turned, Tyler was there by his side. Slowly, Alec had started to believe he always would be. His brothers had been, too, giving him a social outlet he'd lost a long time ago. God, he'd even started to decide what hobbies he wanted to take up to stay busy while Tyler was away.

The moment Tyler's fingers slid out, something a lot bigger pressed into him.

Alec gasped, curling his fingers around the edges of the desk. He pressed his face against it, his ass brushing Tyler's thighs as Tyler sank his cock deep inside.

As blissful as this felt on the rare weekend they spent together, it was all the better after a drought. He panted Tyler's name and shoved back into him, arching his back. "Fuck me," Alec begged. "I need you."

"I will, baby," Tyler breathed out. "Hold on tight."

And then bliss took over—pure and simple.

Tyler braced his forearms on either side of Alec's head. He kissed the back of Alec's neck with surprising tenderness considering the quick, sharp thrusts against and into him.

The time for words was long past. Their language was incoherent groans, smacking skin, gasps for breath, the heat and sweat of their skin pressed together, and above all, the way Tyler's fingers slid into the gaps between Alec's.

How the hell had he ever thought he could do without this?

Alec squeezed Tyler's fingers tightly, grinding against the maddeningly smooth surface of the desk.

"Look at us," Tyler whispered.

Alec resisted, turning his face away. Tyler gently cupped his cheek, turning his head so he looked in the mirror that hung over the bed, and suddenly, Alec couldn't look away.

Tyler's body blanketed Alec's, pressing him firmly against the desk. With every deep, hard thrust, Tyler's cock rubbed inside Alec.

He'd thought that only he could feel the pleasure, but he watched himself ripple, pushing up against Tyler's chest every time the sparks of pleasure danced along his skin.

They looked perfect.

His gaze wandered to Tyler's in the mirror, and Tyler grinned at him, then leaned down to kiss between his shoulder blades. "I might even let you flip over so I can jerk off that hot little cock of yours," Tyler told him.

Alec immediately wriggled under him.

Tyler laughed, pressing him flat against the desk with a hand where his lips had just been. "I didn't say *yet*."

"I did," Alec pouted. "I'm gonna get a mess all over... whatever that is." He hadn't looked twice at the papers under him before grabbing the desk.

"Unless I bring it back to the wall. God, I just wanna do you against every surface<" Tyler growled in his ear.

Alec whimpered at the thought of them screwing on the floor, against the wall, on the bed, against the wardrobe, on the windowsill...

"I figure I've got ten days to make up for," Tyler told him, his voice rough. "This makes one."

Oh, God. How the hell was he gonna sit still in the stands tomorrow? Alec found he didn't care. "Yes!"

The thought sent a wave of heat through him, and he was more desperate than ever for a touch.

Tyler slid out, pulled him upright, and walked him over to the wall before turning his cheek again to make him look back at the mirror.

Alec's gaze flickered between his own cheeks as he felt and saw them burn red, and the thick shaft pressing against him again.

He slid his hands up the wall, digging his nails in as hard

as he dared. "Want you coming inside me, baby," he told Tyler, groaning as Tyler's hand wrapped around his shaft.

With every thrust, Tyler jerked his cock now, hard and fast.

Alec was in heaven, his head spinning as he buckled against the wall, the cold surface a shock to the heat and sweat of his back, and everything from Tyler's chest to his thighs pressed against Alec's back.

"I can't—I'm almost…" He squeezed his eyes shut before forcing himself to open them again and watch himself. Actually seeing Tyler's throbbing cock disappearing into him at the same time as he felt himself filled up was incredibly erotic.

So was watching his own face twist into pleasure as he gasped Tyler's name. Then, it was louder. "Tyler… Ty! Ty, fuck, yes!"

Bliss overtook him as he squeezed around Tyler, and it took him a few moments to notice the break in Tyler's rhythmic thrusts.

He was coming, wrapping Alec in his arms and pressing kisses along his shoulders. "I love you," Tyler breathed out. "I love you, I fuckin' love you, Alec Lands."

Alec slid his hand down the wall to cover Tyler's against his hip, turning his head and kissing Tyler's cheek and lips. "I love you, too, baby."

By the time they stumbled to the bed together, he was still wet and sore and utterly blissful, but considering which furniture looked sturdiest in this room.

"I missed the hell outta you," Tyler murmured, pulling Alec against him. They were face-to-face at last, and Tyler's face had that utterly sincere expression that Alec had fallen for, what felt like so long ago.

"I felt as much. I like this road warrior career you've got going on, if it comes with *these* perks," Alec told him.

Tyler laughed and kissed his forehead, then his nose, and finally, his lips. "These perks are up for the offering. Just say the word."

"Which word is that?"

"Fuck me," Tyler whispered, his voice dropping an octave.

"That's two words."

Tyler eyed him. "Never said I was a genius."

"I still don't believe your denial," Alec informed him, rubbing his chest and nestling his cheek into Tyler's arm. "So there."

Tyler laughed and closed his eyes, running his hand down Alec's side. "I'll have to fuck you face-to-face next so I can kiss you and keep that smart-ass mouth busy."

"Or I could keep *your* smart-ass mouth busy," Alec winked, shoving Tyler's head down lightly.

Tyler laughed and play-wrestled him. Alec could tell he was holding back his strength, which was the sweetest idea, since Alec knew every muscle that could immobilize Tyler. Still, it was the thought that counted.

When Alec ended up on top and triumphant, he beamed down at Tyler. "Love the view. I'm keeping it."

"Good," Tyler smiled back at him and slid his hands above his head in surrender—or perhaps a signal that he was almost ready for another round. His expression was... gentle. Trusting. Loving.

Alec held the silence for a few more moments before he flopped down against Tyler and kissed him.

This is it, Alec thought, a smile creeping across his face. Everything Alec had never known he was looking for... it was right here, in Tyler's arms.

Epilogue

TYLER, DECEMBER

"I FEEL LIKE A HIBERNATING BEAR. I WOKE UP AND THERE WAS snow." Tyler blinked and rubbed his eyes, gazing out the car window.

For a change, Alec was doing the driving and he was in the passenger seat as the snow-capped Smokies unfolded around them.

"Mm? You did sleep for just about two days straight when you came home," Alec told him with a smile.

Tyler reached out to rest his hand on top of Alec's, on the emergency brake. "Thank you for feeding the bear."

Alec grinned. "My pleasure. Bears need plenty of protein. One face-fucking at a time."

Even now, months after moving in with the man, Tyler was still surprised at what came out of Alec's mouth. He burst out laughing and squeezed Alec's hand. "Is that why you're taking me to a cabin?"

"Nah. I'm stealing your kidney. Mr. Top-Ten, Miraculous Comeback, Wonder Boy," Alec teased. "I'm sure I can sell it for a bunch."

"You're not funny," Tyler groused. He hadn't stood a chance of winning after the races he'd missed that summer, but even so, he'd kind of hoped he could pull off some kind of math miracle and manage it.

Top-ten for individual points wasn't bad, though. It was *really* not bad.

"Then why are you laughing?"

Tyler turned his laugh into a cough and covered his mouth, rubbing his cheeks. The idea of his sweet Alec stealing anyone's kidney was utterly ridiculous. "To... uh... to make you feel better about being unfunny."

"Mmm." Alec drummed his fingers on the brake. "Sure. But, to answer your question, this is a romantic Christmas break. Which is why you're not allowed to drive, and I'm not allowed to test your muscle strength. Well, I'm sure I'll do that, but I won't *measure* it."

"Deal," Tyler grinned. He glanced out the window. "Guess we're not renting bikes."

It was Alec's turn to pout, and unfortunately for him, it was an adorable expression. "Ugh. I can't go biking in the snow."

He'd picked up the hobby toward the end of the summer, and it was doing his ass a world of good. Not that it hadn't already been great enough to catch his eye the very first time they'd slept together. Now it was... well, incredibly distracting from any angle.

Living together, and finally being together day and night, had already led to a lot more sex. Tyler was a little surprised they hadn't had chafing problems.

"Aww. No spandex butt for me to admire," Tyler complained. Still, Alec had already figured out several fun things to do with it, so it wasn't a *real* complaint.

A weekend in the mountains together sounded just about the perfect Christmas. Alec was used to spending Christmases alone, so Tyler had invited him to stay with his family. So had several of his brothers.

Alec had countered by suggesting this—a weekend together first, away from family and friends and coworkers and everyone else.

And that sounded pretty damn perfect to Tyler: the two of them, alone together at last, cherishing every precious moment of these couple months before the next racing season started.

Somehow, Tyler had a feeling it was going to be his best yet.

With Alec by his side, how could it not be?

"I DON'T WANT YOU TO BE THE ONE. I JUST WANT A REBOUND."

After getting dumped at his engagement shoot on a dude ranch in Tennessee, Evan's life is falling apart. The ranch owner, Josh, offers him the chance to live and work here for a few months, and Evan jumps on it—and on him.

There's no denying what he feels for Josh, but Evan's not sure if he can trust his heart when it's still broken. Unless it brought him here because he's finally found where he belongs.

Josh has a closet full of skeletons, and even his best friends don't know about some of them. He took over the ranch when his dad died and left it to him—the memories and the guilt came free.

He knows he shouldn't risk his heart if Evan's just here for a good time. But Evan is right for him, and he's perfect for Evan, in ways that he's never even imagined before.

Maybe this sudden passion is exactly what they've both been missing. What if a so-called rebound is exactly what they need to launch them forward into a future—together?

About the Author

E. Davies writes feel-good, low-angst romance that never fades to black when the going gets good! Born in Canada, after 16 moves and counting, Ed has finally put down roots in north London.

He emerges from his writing nest to coo over fuzzy animals, flee from cute guys, dance through the streets with his chosen family, put together fierce looks, and—most of all—befriend local flowers.

You can find all available titles at: www.edaviesbooks.com

FOLLOW E. DAVIES ONLINE:

amazon.com/author/edavies
bookbub.com/authors/e-davies
facebook.com/edaviesauthor
goodreads.com/edavies
instagram.com/edaviesauthor
x.com/edaviesauthor

Sunrise Island Brothers:

Collide

Stranded

Hart's Bay:

Hard Hart

Changed Hart

Wild Hart

Stolen Hart

Significant Brothers:

Splinter

Grasp

Slick

Trace

Clutch

Tremble

Riley Brothers:

Buzz

Clang

Swish

Crunch

Slam

Grind

Brooklyn Boys:

Electric Sunshine

Live Wire

Boiling Point

F-Word:

Flaunt

Freak

Faux

Forever

Freedom

After:

Afterburn

Afterglow

Aftermath

Shared Universes:

Shelter

Adore

Miracle

Redemption

Limelight

Barely Regal